The Confessic

(Or How to Survive a Mi

Lee Ball

Published by YouWriteOn.com, 2011

First Edition

A CIP catalogue record for this title is available from the British Library.

Acknowledgements

Thanks must firstly go to David Pickering for editing the book and for his helpful suggestions and to Ilias Arahovitis for the excellent cover. Thanks must also go to Robert Hastings, Stuart Winfield, The Stanger Family and Adrian Magson – they know why. I must also give a rather large nod to the 'Cheeky Chappie' himself, the great Max Miller.

Finally, huge thanks must also go to my mother and my wife for all their support and encouragement over the years, and of course, whatever I do, I must not forget my two wonderful boys, Jason and Aidan.

Introduction

It's an odd thing, delivering groceries. It's a bit like being an astronaut (bear with me on this one). From blast-off to touch-down I spend most of my time alone. My universe is a small part of England that takes in the beautiful counties of Buckinghamshire and Oxfordshire. I soar to and from the tiny worlds within it – places like the bizarrely named Botolph Claydon and Piddington and Bicester. I'm happy in what I do.

Mainly, I suspect, because I don't venture into that terrifying globular cluster that is Milton Keynes. In my universe there is no darkness. Instead, I marvel at the green lush fields and hills that seamlessly bind the two counties together. It allows me time to think, to wonder at the mystery of it all. Unfortunately, it also gives my imagination time to run riot.

1

Her Name Was Lola

Miss Lola P of Stratton Audley was a very strange cookie indeed. She was of South American extraction and, according to her, a one-time showgirl. Whether she'd ever worn feathers in her hair and a dress cut down to 'there', though, is open to question.

To all the drivers she was less a customer, more an experience. And we were all given the same treatment.

'Darlings!' (we were *all* referred to as 'darlings') 'It is you! My favourite of all the drivvers.'

Yes, you read it correctly, 'drivvers'.

'When you come in your van I am taken into ecstasy!'

She would play with us all. But I can't deny the pleasure I found in being teased by an exotic beauty. Especially on a wet night in North Bucks.

Her weekly delivery could vary, but it mostly consisted of exotic fruit. Well, as exotic as you can get in a Buckinghamshire supermarket. Over time, I wondered what wonderful concoctions she would conjure up after my departure. Was she a genius in the kitchen? Did she create mouth-watering desserts to tempt lonely deliverymen to their doom? Were the fruits juiced up and mixed with hard liquor to create mind-bending cocktails? Or (and forgive me if I am allowing my thoughts to run away with me once more) did she harbour magical powers and form them into figures to bring to life for night-long orgies?

There is, of course, the possibility that she just liked fruit.

The problem was that, thanks to Lola's oddness, it was almost impossible to find out anything about her. I

suppose I was luckier than most. Over time, having pieced together the tiny snippets of information she would reveal, it was possible to peer into her mind. Despite her behaviour, I rather liked Lola.

Her delivery was always at the same time, between nine and eleven on a Wednesday evening, and to all the 'drivvers' she was the highlight of our week. She was a legend, and none of us would ever forget the first delivery to Lola P.

Mine was on a strangely cold summer night, with a northerly wind howling across the landscape. Lola was my final customer that night. There was no moon and barely any street lighting. It was so dark, in fact, that I nearly missed her house, which sat on a ridge above the village. Her home was as dark as the night, and at first I assumed no one was home. Obliged as I was to ring the doorbell, I waited as the wind tugged at my hair. For a moment or two there was no reply, but just as I was about to return to the van with the burgeoning trays of papaya, mango and prickly pear, I heard loud music and saw a thrusting, popping shape approaching the front door. In muted wonder, I watched as it then flew open and I came eye to eye with Lola P for the first time.

'Darlings,' she yelled above the sound of a bossa nova. She was voluptuous, brown and revealing in a low-cut, fiery red, polka-dot dress. 'Follow me, my darlings!'

Like a moth to a flame, I obeyed, my eyes fixed on her gyrating form as it went into the kitchen. I was defenceless to her hypnotic shuffling movement and could do nothing more than watch as she danced around me. As she did, she clapped and yelped and ran her fingers through my hair. Then, as the music stopped, she threw back her head, to reveal a plastic rose clenched between her teeth.

'Is it short?' I heard her mutter.

'I'm sorry,' I replied, not quite sure what she was talking about.

'The order? Is it short?'

'Er, no. Everything's there.'

'Oh, how nice. Now,' she giggled, throwing the rose into the sink and circling me again. 'I have never seen you before! You are a new drivver. I thought I knew all the drivvers, but I don't know you! What do you think of Lola? Do I not excite you? Do I not bring out the demon inside? Don't say a thing! I know it is all too much for you. I know what you are thinking. I can almost see in your mind. Oh, you naughty, naughty man! Oh! How could you think such a thing about little Lola? But wait. Don't be too harsh on yourself. In my presence you have no defences!'

She wasn't wrong either. I had no defence whatsoever. I was bloody terrified. If it hadn't been for the trays I was gripping tightly, I would have been out the door and driving off in the van. That should have been the end of it, but then I went and made a bad situation a whole lot worse.

'Where would you like me to put it?'

'Oh, you naughty boy!'

Oh God

'You're playing with poor Lola! Do what the other drivvers do. Slip it on the table,' she ordered, her back arched across the table. 'But you'll have to take it out for me. I've lost all control!'

I think I can safely say I have never been so astonished in all my life. It was like a Carry On film. I wouldn't have been more surprised if Sid James had jumped out of the fridge.

Over the following months I learned a lot about Lola from her own lips. According to her, she was a dance teacher and was dating an English lord. As soon as his divorce came through, they intended to depart these shores for Rio, where they planned to open the greatest nightclub in South America. As I listened I would smile, aware all the time that she was actually dating a married car salesman from Brackley. I also knew that she was not a dance teacher at all, but a cleaner at a rival store. But never once did I judge Lola. I envied her in a way. She had discovered what the vast majority of us also have to learn – that life is pretty dire when you are alone. Unlike the rest of us, however, she had found a way out.

And in a world of fantasy the possibilities of escape are endless.

I use the past tense when speaking of Lola because a few weeks ago the deliveries stopped. At first, I thought she may have gone on holiday, but as I drove past her house one Sunday afternoon I found it deserted and a 'for sale' sign in the garden. I was at a loss. Why hadn't she mentioned it? Had she fallen victim to the credit crunch?

Or had my information been wrong and she was now Lady Lola, the hostess of the finest nightclub in the southern hemisphere?

Funny that isn't it? Old Lola? What a character. I've got a confession for you. She doesn't exist. I made her up. She's a figment of my rather over-fertile, middle-aged imagination. It is possible, I suppose, that I based her on someone I've delivered to or met in my dark and distant past, but the truth of it is, there is no Lola.

I *am* a delivery driver you see, and over the past few years I've made up quite a lot of stories about non-existent customers. But why would a grown man do such a thing, I hear you ask? And that's a very good point. Why would I?

I think I need to explain a few things.

I've been driving a van now for three years. When I began, I resented having to take on such a mundane job. You see, I used to be an actor. Back then, I had dreams of winning Oscars and Baftas and the attention of beautiful women. But fate had other plans and before I knew it I was delivering groceries for a well-known supermarket. Now I can look back and smile, but at the time I didn't see the world in such a positive light. I was at a low ebb – I suppose you could call it a mid-life crisis.

I had hoped by the time I was forty I'd be a household name, a star of TV and film. Instead, I was a househusband working from home. Where, I asked myself, did it all go wrong? Then a couple of years later I started a new job as a driver. And that's how this all began.

2

Granada Here I Come

A couple of years after leaving Drama College I was ill. Out of nowhere, I had a series of epileptic fits, which, of course, is not good for an actor. I went to see a neurologist. She was very sympathetic and straight to the point.

'You're now officially an epileptic.'

'Thank you very much,' I said, trying to keep the moment light.

'What's your profession?'

'I'm an actor.'

'Oh dear.'

'I know. There's not much work, but the money's good,' I said, trying to keep the moment even lighter.

'I'm afraid that until we find out why you're having these attacks, you'll have to stop for a while.'

'How long is a while?'

'A year ... two years. For as long as it takes really. Do you drive?'

'I do.'

'I'm afraid you'll have to stop that as well.'

It was getting worse by the second. I tried another joke. 'What about sex? Might even enhance it, I expect?'

It didn't work. Despite my levity, I was very shaken. This was serious. I just couldn't take it all in.

'Are you working at the moment?' she asked, her eyes now adopting a sorrowful quality.

'No,' I replied.

It was true, technically.

What I didn't tell her was that I had just landed a part in *Coronation Street*. First scene? Driving a car down the famous cobbles and parking outside that most famous of pubs.

On the way home from the hospital, I decided I was far too ashamed (and far too skint) to inform Granada Television. How could I explain that the actor they had employed only a month before had since become a break-dancer?

Within a few days I was back at the hospital, undergoing a series of tests. The result? It seemed the fits stemmed from a head injury in my youth. Suddenly, everything began to make sense. For years, even on stage, I'd been experiencing odd sensations. I realised now that they were petit mals and, in a way, discovering what they were and why they were happening was quite a relief.

Having to put my career on hold to sort it out, however, was not.

A week later I was at Granada Studios, in Manchester. For a young actor fresh out of Drama College it was a daunting moment. But I had bigger concerns. What would happen if I had a fit on the set? I would never work again. My acting career would be over in a week. You see, because it was early on in the investigation, the doctors were uncertain what type of medication to put me on. So, at the beginning, I wasn't put on anything. I was a walking time bomb – I could blow at any second. And what if the neurologist saw my performance a month later and contacted the DVLA? It was a worrying time.

'You must be Lee,' said a pretty young assistant. I nodded nervously as she led me off to costume and make-up, before introducing me to the other actors.

There before me were faces I had seen a thousand times: Julie Goodyear, Bill Tarmey, Johnny Briggs, Eva Pope, Bill Roach and the others. I was aware of them but, of course, they didn't have a clue who I was. At the end of the week I would be gone and forgotten. Unless, of course, I had a fit in the green room, or, God forbid, on the set itself. *Then* I would be remembered for all time. 'Do you remember that Lee, the one that played the detective?' 'The one that had the fit and devastated Betty's hotpot? How could I forget? The bastard!'

The more I thought about things, the worse it got. All day sitting amongst those iconic figures – I became more and more terrified.

'Don't have a fit. Don't have a fit,' I said to myself over and over.

For most of the day everything was fine. I was almost shaking with fear, but somehow I kept it together. Then came the call.

'Lee?' It was the pretty young assistant again. 'They're ready for you on set.'

Smiling nervously, I got to my feet and followed her outside to meet the director.

'Hello there. Look, we're a bit behind, so if you could just follow my assistant Tom, he'll show you what I want you to do.'

'Fine,' I said, trying my best to sound as relaxed as I could.

Following young Tom up the street, the fear began to overtake me in such a way that I was having difficulty doing the basics. Things like walking in a straight line, swallowing and breathing, that sort of thing. Then I saw The Rovers and things got a whole lot worse.

'It's a BMW,' said Tom.

'I'm sorry?' I replied, my eyes fixed on the famous frontage.

'The car you'll be driving. Have you ever driven one?'

I shook my head. Even though I'd passed my test six years earlier, I'd only driven half a dozen times or so. My problems were magnifying by the moment. Eventually, I think I muttered something about being a competent driver and walked to the car.

'What we want you to do is just slowly drive round the corner and park directly outside The Rovers. Do you think you could do that?'

'Fine,' I said, even though in my head I had visions of getting in the car, having a fit and driving *through* The Rovers.

Apart from a couple of stalls and an embarrassing moment where I nearly ran over the director, all went well. All I had to do now was my scene in The Rovers and I could go home. The trouble was, that was not until the end of the week and, sitting in the green room with all of those stars, and remaining convinced that I was going to have a fit at any second, was hardly what you might call conducive to a competent performance.

And so, on a Friday evening sometime in the early nineties, I gave possibly the worst performance any young actor delivered in a soap. I was so nervous by then that my voice was about forty octaves higher than it should have been. I was so wooden you could have extended The Rovers bar with me. When I saw the performance a month or so later, it only confirmed my fears. I wanted to go back and do it again. I wanted to prove that I was a bloody good actor, one of the first in his year to be signed up by an agent. But until I got the all-clear from the doctors, I couldn't do a bloody thing.

That was where all my problems began. While waiting for the all-clear, doubt crept in. Like glue it held me down. Before long I was wallowing in self-pity. Now I didn't want to be an actor. I wanted seclusion. I wanted to be left alone.

'When you going back to acting then?' or 'Any work in the pipeline?' were questions that filled me with fear and I went to great lengths to avoid answering them.

It was around this time that I started to write. Having appeared in a couple of (very bad) short films, I had decided to write screenplays. I then progressed to novels. My first was called *The Immortal Miss Jude* ... catchy title, eh? Well, the publishers didn't seem to think so. Like a bad penny, it came back again and again.

But I don't give up easy, me. No, I wrote another. It was called *God's Will* ... catchy title, eh? Well ... you know the rest.

It was at this time that I came to the conclusion that I was probably not cut out to be an artist.

Months turned into years and before I knew it I had accumulated a wife, two children, a job working from home and rather a large mortgage. I should have been happy, and I was, but there was this little voice in my head repeating over and over. Failure. Failure. Failure.

'Get a grip of yourself – you're not dying, you whingeing arse!' my wife said. The Scots tell it like it is. And, of course, she was right. But pain is relative and mine was like an overbearing aunt with large bosoms.

On my forty-second birthday, I looked back on my life. I didn't like what I saw. It got worse a week later. My cushy job working from home came to a sudden end. This was a major problem. You see I was – and still am – a househusband. Working from home was perfect for looking after the kids. Where the hell was I going to get another job like that?

My wife duly noted this.

'What are you going to do now?'

It was clear she wasn't going to go 'on the game'. Speech therapists are worked so hard these days, they simply don't have time for moonlighting. I needed another job. And quick. As chance would have it, we were having our groceries delivered that day, courtesy of a well-known supermarket.

'How are you today?' said the driver.

'Piss off,' I replied.

Luckily, he was smaller than me and had not only a sense of humour but interesting news. It seemed they were short of delivery drivers and were desperate for someone to start soon.

As my wife and I put away the shopping, she went out of her way to remind me of how much we needed the money. I knew then I had no choice. The epilepsy was in the past and I had a clean driving licence. But did I really want to become a delivery driver? What would my acting friends think? Well considering I'd lost contact with most of them, and I hadn't acted for years, it didn't seem that relevant anymore. So I applied, did the standard driving test and got the job.

Little did I know what I was letting myself in for.

3

Home Shopping Here I Come

So one week after my moment of providence with the deliveryman, I was driving a van for a supermarket. For the first couple of shifts I went out with another driver just to get a feel of the job. Not that delivering groceries is that difficult. It normally works in this order.

1. Load the van with groceries.
2. Drive the van to the customer's house.
3. Give the customer their groceries.
4. Return when you have no groceries left.

Rocket science, it ain't.

At first the job was a breeze. With my trusty sat nav securely attached to the windscreen, I delivered with confidence and a smile. But then I began to meet some of the more bizarre customers. Now I'm a pretty easy going bloke, but some of these people would test the patience of a saint.

Take the incident in my first week for instance.

One day I got lost. For some reason the sat nav seemed to freeze. It was a scary moment. I pulled over and checked the map. Still no good. So I did the only sensible thing. I rang the customer for directions. She asked me where I was and I told her – in a country lane near a railway track. What she said next was ridiculous, but also, in its own way, a catalyst for writing this book.

'We live near a tree,' she said.

No, really.

I asked her to be a little more specific. It all went quiet and I sensed only a little of the confusion was mine. You see, if she'd told me that she was living in the old stationmaster's house up the line, which she was, it would have saved me fifteen minutes driving around looking at every tree on the outskirts of Bicester.

Trust me. It's not easy for a delivery driver.

Trees indeed.

4

Depression Here I Come

At the end of my first week of employment, I was sitting in the deserted staff canteen, staring up blankly at the television. I remember the moment clearly. It was a Friday night and the usual trailers were showing for the weekend cinema. It was then that I saw a familiar face on the screen, an old friend from college. I knew Kevin McKidd had done well – I'd seen him in various TV shows over the years, but now he was in Hollywood, starring in movies. I pinched myself to make sure I wasn't having a nightmare. There was I working in a supermarket, whilst an old pal was living it up in Hollywood. Come on then, life, what else you got? Why not have my worst enemy win the Booker Prize, you bastard!

I felt I couldn't get any lower. My fall was complete. I was in my mid-forties and had been out of the acting profession for nearly fifteen years. I suppose, deep down inside, I had a faint hope that there would be a phone call out of the blue and I would get back. But that night in a deserted staff canteen in Buckingham, I realised I had blown my chances for all time. What made it worse was realising that I was a failure because I hadn't had the guts to go back and have another try. Within weeks I had thrown my toys out of the pram and I was sulking on an epic scale.

During the next week I went to great lengths to block out all negative thought. I even devised a game to make it more bearable. I called it 'guess the customer'. It's simple to play. All you need to do is guess the customer's shape and personality from their order.

My first customer was Mr E of Bicester. His order told me a lot. Eight large tins of sausage and beans, one family-sized box of Crunchy Nut Cornflakes, one large pack of jam iced doughnuts and twenty-four cans of bargain lager (amongst other cholesterol-soaked items) gave me a fair indication of the condition of his heart for starters. As I waited at the door I tried to visualise Mr E in my mind. Slowly a figure grew in the darkness. A very fat man with a prematurely bald head. He could have been any age between forty and eighty.

The door opened. Sadly, I was correct in every way. Mr E is single and, from the reddish tint that has blossomed around his nose and cheeks, a stranger to vegetables and fruit.

This is as far as I am willing to go, though, because in his sad, empty eyes I see a bit of myself. But whereas I have a loving wife and family to keep me from the precipice, Mr E has no one. On this particular doorstep I have found a man unloved, hiding from the world on a diet that will take him from it sooner than he realises. Maybe this is his plan. Maybe he's reached some silent conclusion that tells him there is more happiness to be found in his weekly groceries than in his fellow man. Apart from the usual pleasantries, he doesn't speak much, but I know from his forced smile and simple dignity that there was once love in Mr E's life. Now he is alone, living on a time bomb of carbohydrates and vitamin deficiency. Poor Mr E.

For those first few weeks, I lived in a dream. Every day was the same. Drive, park, unload. Over and over. Bicester, Buckingham, Brackley, Bucknell. From time to time, questions would surface in my mind. Like, what have I done with my life? Why can't I have a little bit of success? And why do all the towns around here begin with B? On top of this, I was beginning to get a little pissed off with the inane comments of my customers.

'Looks like we are in for a bit of weather.' What the hell does that mean?

Things picked up at the end of the first month. I actually got a tip.

'Ere you are, mate, get yourself a drink.'

'Thank you,' I replied, wondering what sort of drink I could get for fifty pence.

I was in a living hell. I *was* a spaceman, on a one-way mission to nowhere. Inevitably, I began to make comparisons between the customers and myself, each night going home feeling as lonely and as empty as poor Mr E.

At the end of that first month, it all came to a head. It was my night off and I was watching an old episode of *The Sweeney* (when we men are down we revert to our youth). My wife was talking about the upheavals in the NHS and how hard her job had become, but Mr Selfish wasn't listening. Instead, he was trying to shut out the world by watching Jack Regan knock six colours of the brown stuff out of a couple of 'slags'. Then she went and said it.

'I see Kevin (McKidd) is in that new Ridley Scott film.'

Could she not sense my isolation? What was she thinking of? I won't go into all the sordid details, but from there we embarked on the mother of all arguments. After the tears had dried – my wife seemed okay – we talked for a while and, for the first time in a long time, I explained the real root of my problems. Not getting published and working for a supermarket were at the top of the list.

'If you think it's bad driving a van, you want to come and work for the NHS. Maybe you could write about it. Or don't you stretch to tragedies?'

Then something clicked in my head. Why hadn't I thought of it before? To my knowledge, nobody had written a book on home delivery. That was it, my road to Damascus moment. With my genius for the witty quip, combined with my penetrating insight (not to mention modesty) how could it fail? Maybe there *was* a way of becoming a success. Yes, from the ashes of failure, I would rise like a phoenix of hope. I would be a shining example of British doggedness, I would … well, you get the general idea.

5

The Deliveryman's Revenge

For the first time in my life I was actually looking forward to doing a hard day's work. Studying the route before each run, I could only wonder at what extraordinary experiences I was about to have. In my head, there was so much potential for stories – sex-starved housewives, mad professors, funny pets and cheeky children, or, even, sex-starved professors, mad housewives, funny children and cheeky pets. I was so excited!

Knocking at each door, I waited and hoped that something marvellous would happen. The trouble was, nothing did. Before I knew it, my newfound enthusiasm had disappeared and the depression had returned. Instead of larger-than-life figures, I was getting unhappy people, rude people, lonely people, every kind of people but the ones I wanted. Not only did I have the wrong cast - the one I had wasn't even following the bleedin' script. Nothing was happening. It was awful.

My wife suggested I see the doctor. I was less than enthusiastic – he was getting on a bit and had a habit of forgetting you completely from one appointment to the next. But, telling myself he was the one who had helped me when I was diagnosed with epilepsy, I decided it might be worth a visit.

'I think you're having a mid-life crisis,' he announced after listening to my whingeing for a minute or so. He had a glass eye and I could never decide which one to focus on, so I stared at his forehead instead. 'It's quite common for men of your age. It's that big four 'O', you see? To some men it's nothing, but to others, men like yourself, it's like a big mirror forcing you to see your faults and your failings.'

'Yes, thanks for that, doc.'

'What do you do, if you don't mind me asking?' he added.

'Through the day I'm a househusband ...'

'I see. Reversed roles, eh? I recall reading a paper on that a few years ago. There were some fascinating findings.'

I was intrigued.

'What like?'

'Well, the man resenting the wife for being the main earner, the shame of taking on the female role, the attack on his masculinity, the guilt that the man is no longer providing for his family, that sort of thing. Have you ever considered any of that?'

'I hadn't until now.'

'There's probably nothing in it,' he added, as if he was talking about the weather. 'Do you do anything else?'

'Yes, actually I do,' I said, angrily, 'in the evening I'm a delivery driver.'

'I see. Have you always done this?'

'No. I used to be an actor.'

'Ah!' he said, slapping the desk. 'There we have it. No doubt there's still a part of you that longs to tread the boards, eh? Without the smell of grease paint and an audience, your life must seem pretty drab. Why did you stop, if you don't mind me asking?'

'I became an epileptic?' I reminded him.

'Ooh! You shouldn't be driving if you're an epileptic.'

'I'm no longer an epileptic. I've been cleared by the DVLA. You wrote the letter.'

'I did?' he said. 'Oh yes, of course, how silly of me. And how is life treating you?'

'Not great ... that's why I'm here.'

'Yes, yes, of course. Look, my suggestion is don't worry about things. Just try and get on the best way you can. Try and keep your mind occupied. Do you have a hobby?'

'I write,' I said.

'Good. What sort of things?'

'Novels, mainly.'

'That's exactly the sort of distraction you need. Keep at it. Never give in. That's what my father used to say to me. Never give in.'

'Was your father a doctor too?'

'My father? Never knew my father. He died when I was very young, you know.'

I was too tired and confused to continue so I just got up and walked to the door. But he beat me to it.

'Now don't worry,' he said, patting me on the back. 'It's just a phase. Just remember everything I said and keep taking the tablets.'

'What tablets?'

'Eh? No, I don't mean tablets, do I? I mean advice. The advice I gave you. Take plenty of it and you'll be fit as a fiddle before you know it. Good day!'

As the door closed, I sensed the world was conspiring against me. Why are there so many mad people in my life, I asked myself? It was then I remembered the woman who lived in the old stationmaster's house. I don't know why I thought about her, maybe because of her mad comment about the tree. But the more I thought about her, the more my imagination took over. Then it dawned on me. I wouldn't wait for the stories to come along. I would make them up!

Within half an hour I had turned an experience into a story.

6

Signs of Life

Had a few problems with my sat nav the other day. For some reason it sent me to a deserted lane. Well, I say deserted – there were a couple of rabbits, but unless they'd bought a laptop and opened a bank account, I had a feeling the delivery wasn't for them.

So I did the only sensible thing, I called the customer direct.

'Hello,' said a loud, pompous man.

'Hello, I've got a delivery for you, but I'm having a few problems finding you.'

'Oh, this is always happening! Are you in a lane?'

'Yes.'

'Are there lots of rabbits?'

'Yes, there are.'

'Is there a poplar?'

'A what?'

'A tree, man ... a tree! A poplar!'

'Er, yes … a small one.'

'Does it look like a letter Y?'

'What?'

'The tree ... does it look like a letter Y?'

'I suppose so. Mind you, at a certain angle I suppose it could pass as a T.'

'Yes, I know the one ... you've gone too far.'

Conversations like these are common. It seems the general public have perfected the art of wasting my time.

'Now what you need to do is turn around ... drive a mile until you see a bush on your left that looks a little like David Gest...'

I paused, unsure if I've heard him correctly.

'Sorry, did you say David Gest?'

'That's right.'

'The American?'

'That's the chappy … you'll see what I mean when you see it ... it's quite round with odd little bushy bits all over it.'

'Is there another one near it that looks like Liza Minnelli?'

'Don't be silly!'

He seemed quite cross at my levity, so I changed my tone. 'So what do I do when I see Mr Gest?'

'You carry on for another mile, until you see a gate on your right.'

'What does the gate look like?'

'It looks like a gate, you damned fool. What else would it look like?'

Thanking him for his rather odd, but bizarrely precise directions, I did a tight three-point-turn (careful not to squash a rabbit) and drove off.

I drove and I drove. On the way I saw many trees and bushes. Although one of them (a bedraggled holly bush) had a look of a girl I used to go out with, I decided none of them bore any resemblance to that strangest of Americans.

I called the customer back.

'Hello!'

'Sorry ... still having a few problems finding you.'

'What about David Gest?'

'Must have missed him.'

'Bugger ... mind you, it is summer now. I suppose he looks different with leaves.'

'I expect so. What now then?'

'Did you see the gate?'

'No.'

'Well, we're not doing very well at all, are we? What did we order again?'

'A couple of cases of wine,' I said, looking down at his receipt.

'Oh, is that all? Tell you what ... stay where you are and I'll come and find you.'

And before I could say a thing he'd rung off. Realising there was nothing I could do but sit and wait, I got out of the van and wallowed in the afternoon sun beating down onto the fields and woods all around. If only all my customers would do this, I thought to myself. But before I could get too engrossed in thought, I noticed a cloud of billowing dust coming towards me along the parched road.

'Hello there! You went right past us,' said an elderly head poking out of opened window of the four-by-four. 'We're a mile or so back. Don't blame yourself though. A few years ago, we had a chap who got stuck up old Guinevere...'

Now, I know I shouldn't have asked ... but I simply had to know.

' Guinevere? Is that a bush?'

'A dyke.'

It was then that I decided to end my line of enquiry. Sometimes it's better not to know all the details.

I can't begin to tell you how refreshing it is turning a negative moment into a comical one. It's a bit like playing God. I was adjusting the past until it worked in my favour. And this was only the start.

7

Battered and Bruised

Now I had a plan to get ahead, my outlook on life changed for the better. I was so excited. My mind was like a tinderbox. All I needed was a spark, a comment, a phrase, an odd inflection, or, if I was really lucky, a nutcase. Unfortunately for me most people tend not to be nutcases. Most of my customers are like you and I. Of course, when I say this, I'm presuming you're not a deranged madman. But, occasionally, if I'm lucky, I deliver to someone who is just plain odd.

One Sunday I delivered to a lady who, when discovering her frozen Yorkshire puddings were out of stock, 'lost it' on the doorstep. The woman was clearly bonkers. I mean what sort of person loses their temper over Yorkshire puddings? Under normal circumstances I would have probably lost my temper too. But now I had made the decision to write about my experiences, everything was different.

*   *   *   *

Yesterday I was in Bicester. Even though I don't live in Bicester, I seem to spend most of my time there. I only had a couple of deliveries to go as I knocked on the door of Mrs P of Parkhaven Road. She was a scary, orange-coloured woman with even scarier hair. Passing her invoice from a safe distance, I explained the only thing unavailable was her frozen Yorkshire puddings.

Oddly, this minor detail turned Mrs P into a wild woman. That's right. Now she was wild and scary.

'What am I going to do?' she yelled, her long hair almost reaching out for my throat. 'My husband's at

work and I've got my in-laws coming in an hour. How can I give them a Sunday roast without Yorkshire pudding?'

For a moment I just looked at her. There was plenty I wanted to say. The trouble was that most of it could have got me the sack. You see, I like my food the natural way. So you can only imagine my disgust at having to deliver such things as frozen Yorkshire puddings, not too mention frozen roast potatoes. I decided to show Mrs P there was a better way.

'Have you got any flour?' I heard myself say.

'Flour?' she snapped.

'Flour.'

'Somewhere. Why?'

'Do you have any eggs?'

'Eggs?'

'Bear with me. Do you have any eggs?'

'I think so.'

'Do you have an oven?' I must admit there I was taking the 'proverbial'.

'Of course I've got an oven, you cheeky sod! Look, what are you getting at? I've got guests coming round in less than an hour.'

'Well, I was just thinking that you might make your own?'

'Make my own. MAKE MY OWN!'

To be honest, it was a bloody silly suggestion. In her delivery she had frozen roast potatoes, frozen microwaveable roast beef in its own gravy, and frozen carrots and sprouts. Now maybe you can appreciate how my suggestion of actually cooking something must have put the fear of God in her.

In that moment I think I felt a pang of sympathy for Mrs P. Of course, it was mixed with a certain amount of guilt for making the suggestion in the first place, but it was there nevertheless. It was probably this that made me do what I did next.

'Have you got a muffin tray?' I muttered, politely.

'Are you being rude?' she replied, clearly confused.

I realised then she had probably never come across such a thing.

'Look, who are you - Chris Tarrant? What's with all the questions?'

'I was just going to suggest that if you have one ... I could come back in twenty minutes when I've finished ... and ... well ... make the Yorkshire puddings for you.'

'Would you?'

'It would be my pleasure,' I said.

Giving her a list of ingredients, I got in the van and drove off. In that moment I genuinely thought I'd done a good thing. I thought helping my fellow man (or, in this case, scary woman with scary hair) would make me a better person.

Little did I know what hell I had just let myself in for.

Twenty minutes later I returned. I really should have been back at the store at that point, but instead I was following a wild mop of black hair along a narrow hallway into an even narrower kitchen.

'You'll find everything there,' she muttered. 'Eggs, milk and flour – is plain all right?'

'Fine ... and the muffin tray?'

'I'm going to get that now. My friend Belinda's got one. She owes me a favour. She's had my Rabbit for a month.'

Realising she wasn't talking about small furry mammals, I smiled sheepishly. Even though I'm a man of the world, I still managed to blush. And this was a woman who was offended by the words 'muffin tray'. Blimey.

'I won't be long,' she said finally, picking up her car keys. 'The oven's on so get a move on. They'll be here in forty minutes. Oh, and make sure you don't trouble my darlings.'

'Your darlings?'

'Jordan and Peter. Whowhooooo!' she suddenly howled. 'Here you are, my little sweetie pies!'

As she stooped down to greet her little 'darlings', her 'little sweetie pies', I looked down in horror. There, sitting at the kitchen door, were two fat, ugly balls of hate staring up at me. I don't know what breed of dog they were. But that was the least of my concerns. All I was aware of was their teeth. Oh, and what teeth.

'Look after 'em, won't you?' the woman shouted as she darted down the hall.

'No problem,' I muttered to myself. 'No problem at all.'

Making great Yorkshire puds is very simple. You just have to make sure you have equal measures of all your ingredients. It doesn't matter how little or how much mixture there is ... just so long as everything is in equal amounts. So, with this tried and tested theory in mind, I tentatively searched the tiny space for a jug. Of course, I did this with one eye on the dogs, which, like sentinels, remained motionless in the doorway. It took me a while, but eventually I found an old plastic measuring jug and a cup. As I poured the ingredients into the jug, I glanced through a wide serving hatch above the worktop into a largish dining room. When I was done, I turned to find a fork to mix my mix (as it were). I then turned back to pick up the batter, only to discover it was gone.

I looked over at the dogs, but they hadn't moved. In fact, they hadn't taken their ugly eyes off me since I had arrived. I searched the worktop. No. The batter had simply vanished. It was then, as I searched again, that I became aware of a shape through the serving hatch. With a jolt, I realised that someone was watching me. I looked up to see an old man in the dining room, holding (unless I was very much mistaken) a jug of batter mix.

'Hello there,' he said. Despite his tall, frail body, his smile was broad, almost childlike.

'Hello,' I said cautiously.

'Are you a friend of my daughter?'

'Sort of,' I said, with relief. Up until then I had thought he was a ghost.

'Now, you're not a local chap are you?' he said, evidently noting my accent.

'No,' I smiled, 'I'm from Manchester.'

'Ah ... are you a red or a blue?'

'Neither ... I'm a Bolton Wanderers fan.'

'Well,' he said, with a chortle, 'somebody has to be, I suppose.'

On that, he turned and walked out ... with my batter mix.

'Excuse me,' I said. 'EXCUSE ME!'

I said these final two words much too loud and in an instant the dogs were shuffling over to me. Frozen to the spot, I stared down as they sniffed at my ankles.

'Keep it together,' I muttered to myself. 'Keep it together.'

This approach seemed to work because, after a moment or two, they wandered back to their posts by the door.

'Hello there,' said a voice, close by.

'Jesus!'

It was the old man again. Somehow he had reappeared at the serving hatch, scaring the life out of me in the process.

'Sorry ... you gave me a bit of a surprise there,' I said, leaning against the worktop and catching my breath.

'Now, you're not a local chap are you? Are you a friend of my daughter?'

'Er ... yes. As I say, I'm from Manchester.'

'Ah ... are you a red or a blue?'

'Neither ... I'm a Bolton Wanderers fan, remember?'

'Well,' he said, with a chortle, 'somebody has to be.'

In an instant, he was gone again ... with the batter mixture. This time, I somehow managed to control myself and didn't shout out. Nevertheless, I realised I had problem. Not only had I lost the mixture, I was also trapped in the smallest kitchen in England.

It was clear there was only one way of resolving the situation. I had to get the mixture back and get out of there. But that was easier said than done. The only way out of the kitchen was past the dogs ... unless, of course, I went through the serving hatch? Deciding on the latter, I slowly climbed onto the worktop and pushed myself into the dining room.

With no sign of the dogs, I searched the downstairs rooms. It seemed the old man had simply disappeared. Maybe he was a ghost. I checked the garden. Nothing. Maybe he'd gone upstairs? Slowly I made my way back into the house.

'Hello,' I called. 'Are you up there?'

By then I was standing at the foot of the stairs.

'It's the Bolton Wanderers fan ... I was just wondering if I could have my jug back?'

'Now, you're not a local chap are you...'

'Christ!' Somehow the old bugger had appeared behind me. 'Could you please stop doing that!'

Before I could say another word, I was simultaneously aware of two things – the jug of batter mixture in his hand and the dogs, which had appeared from the kitchen to investigate the noise.

'Oh, are these your dogs?' the old man asked, his blank smile as constant as ever.

I wanted to say something, but somehow I stopped myself. I didn't want him to hear my accent again. As I stared at him. with the dogs growling at my feet, I heard a key in the door. Mrs P was back.

'Everything all right? You all right, dad?' she said as I took the batter jug from the old man's wrinkled hand. 'Don't mind him,' she whispered to me. 'He's just a bit forgetful.'

A bit?

Then I noticed the muffin tray in her hand … and a large, shiny Rabbit vibrator in the other. I tried not to look, which was easier said than done (it was eye-wateringly large).

'Right, I'll put the dogs in the garden, so you can get on. How long do you think it will take?'

'Well, if I put them in now, you could keep them warm in the oven for about half an hour.'

'And what about the meat and veg?' she said, letting the dogs out.

'Well, you can do them when you want,' I muttered.

'Me?' she said, reappearing in the hall. 'I've got to get ready. You couldn't be a love and do it for me, could you? All you've got to do is stick 'em in the microwave.'

'But I've got to get back...'

'Oh, go on, be a love ... I'll ring your supervisor and tell him how great you've been.'

'It's a her...'

'Well, I'll ring her,' she said, fluttering her eyelashes.

Of course, I should have told her where to shove her frozen produce, but that just isn't me.

'All right. I'll do the puddings, I'll do the meat and veg and I'll stick it all in the oven for you, but then I'm off.'

'What a lovely man you are,' she said, climbing the stairs and leaving me and her father as she had found us.

'Oh, hello. Are you a friend of my daughter?'

Knowing better than to get into that particular loop again, I returned to the kitchen and prepared the lunch. Within ten minutes I had everything in bowls ready to go into the microwave. All that was left was the puddings. But as I turned to pick up the jug, I saw Mrs P's father through the serving hatch, jug in hand.

'PUT ... THE JUG ... DOWN, OLD MAN!'

'I was just mixing it for you,' he muttered.

'Well, now you've mixed it ... WALK AWAY!'

I don't enjoy shouting at the elderly, but it seemed to do the trick and within seconds he was gone. Almost in the same moment the front door bell rang.

'Could you get that, love!' cried Mrs P from upstairs.

The bloody woman.

Despite my feelings towards their host, I let the guests in and within five minutes the house was full. Avoiding awkward conversation, I hid in the kitchen while the food cooked and Mrs P beautified herself. She seemed to take forever. Probably doing her hair.

Eventually she reappeared, like the Queen of Sheba.

'Okay love, serve it up.'

'What? I've got to go!'

'Oh, never mind all that. You must be famished ... you can stay for lunch.'

'I haven't got time...'

'Of course you have. If your boss complains, I'll explain. By the way, have you seen my Rabbit? I haven't seen it since I came back. I don't want my in-laws finding it.'

Oh, I see, I thought bitterly. She doesn't mind embarrassing me with her frank and open attitude towards self-satisfaction, but when it comes to the family, she's Snow White!

'Anyway,' she continued, 'start serving when you're ready.'

To be honest, by this time I was pretty hungry so, reluctantly, I agreed. Placing the food on the long dining table (with no help of any type, I hasten to add), I was offered a place at the head of the table. After much shouting and screaming, the in-laws came in. For a moment or two, everyone looked at me. Uncles, aunts, grandchildren, nieces.

'Everyone,' said Mrs P, proudly, 'say hello to my delivery driver ... it is he who has cooked this lovely meal. And would you just look at those Yorkshire puddings! Believe it or not, he actually cooked them from scratch.'

There was a collective gasp of astonishment from around the table.

'That's right. He cooked them with raw ingredients. Isn't it amazing what some people can do?'

I smiled, timidly.

'Now, if you would just say 'grace', love.'

It was a moment or two before I realised she was talking to me. I simply didn't know what to do. I've never said 'grace' in my life. I glanced around for help, but every head was bowed and hands were joined around the table. I began to mutter something about us all being thankful, but as I did so something caught my eye. Glancing above the bowed heads, I could see Mrs P's shiny Rabbit perched on the very edge of the serving hatch. From the kitchen, I couldn't see it, but from the dining room it was like a shiny beacon of sexuality. The only thing was ... it was no longer shiny. Now it was yellow ... batter-coloured, to be more precise.

I looked to the far end of the table to see my smiling elderly friend. The old bugger had mixed the batter all right ... with his daughter's dildo. Mind you, in his defence, he probably thought it was a time-saving device, which technically, I suppose it is.

Then I had another thought, one that made me see him in a different light. Maybe he didn't have Alzheimer's at all. Maybe this was him having a bit of fun in his retirement. Either way, his actions had a negative effect on my appetite. With a loud 'Amen' I got up to leave.

'What about your food?' said Mrs P.

'Have it for your supper ... I gotta go.'

'That's not a local accent,' I heard a familiar voice say as I hurried down the hall.

But this time I didn't reply. I was too busy running out of the door to my van.

As I wrote this story I realised how the job was changing my outlook on life. There may be no Mrs P, but there are a lot like her. They tell you things. They share their secrets with you. They ask for advice. Over the years I've become an agony aunt without the boobs and the lipstick.

Up until getting the job I'd never considered what went on behind other peoples closed doors. Or how different or similar we all are. It was as if I was making some type of sociological study, albeit one with characters more suited to a Carry On film.

Something else occurred to me during this time. Would the day ever come where delivered to a publisher?

8

Cucumber Sandwiches

Now my love for writing was reborn, I began to send out my first two novels to publishers. It was a very exciting time, so much so that I introduced the fact that I was a writer into the conversation at every opportunity.

A few weeks after my experience with the Yorkshire pudding woman, I found myself lost again. As you'll discover I get lost a lot. This particular customer was posh with a capital P and by the time I got to his house, the wind had picked up and it was pouring down. The house was huge and set in its own grounds in the middle of nowhere. Unfortunately, I had to park quite a distance from the entrance, which, of course, meant me getting very wet.

And what did the customer do? Pour himself a glass of wine and laugh with his friends as I struggled through the atrocious conditions. I felt like telling the snobby bugger what I thought of him, but I needed the money, so I didn't. It also occurred to me that for all I knew he may have been a publisher. He certainly looked smug enough. Turns out he wasn't.

The delivery took ages and I got very behind … I also got very wet. But, thanks to my imagination, I managed to turn the situation into an altogether more entertaining one.

* * * *

Yesterday it rained. The clouds hung so low I sensed they were reaching out for me. Wherever I went in my little van, the rain was waiting. A sort of liquid ambush, if you will.

Because of the weather, I was way ahead of myself. If there's a world record for hurriedly getting in and out

of vans, I probably hold it. With only one delivery to go, I was half an hour ahead. I didn't know the place. Unfortunately, neither did my sat nav. I pulled over. When situations like this arise, the only sensible thing to do is give the customer a ring. I was greeted with the plummiest voice I have ever heard in my life.

'Hello. Lost you say? Well, well, well. Let my pass you over to me other half. GLORIA!' the voice yelled, almost deafening me. 'GLORIA! Ah, there you are. I've got a delivery chappy on the phone. Wants to know where we live. I'll pass you over, old chap. We're having a bit of a soiree and I'm slightly worse for wear. Don't know me arse from me elbow. Toodle-pip!'

His wife came to the phone to give me directions. Following them to the letter, I found that the address was a manor house at the end of a very long, narrow track on the outskirts of Bicester. The rain was now heavier than ever, and the sky darker than I could have imagined for two o'clock in the afternoon. As I turned onto a long drive of shingle, I was suddenly filled with horror. There, under a huge canopy on the lawn before the house, were a hundred or so people waving at me.

Oh God.

There was nowhere to park but right at the entrance of the house, so I pulled up and jumped out into the rain. No sooner had I done so than I heard a collective cry from the crowd for me to join them all in the tent. I tried to indicate the delivery in the back of the van, but I was outnumbered and in seconds I was running through the raindrops, drawn on by their enthusiasm. I arrived to be greeted with a huge cheer and a cucumber sandwich.

'Good man,' said a familiar voice. It was the toodle-pip man again. 'I see you made it. I knew you would. You seem the type. Good British stock and all that. The name's Gerald.'

Gerald had a maroon face and a long grey band of whiskers that stretched from one ear to the other, only deviating to skirt beneath a bulbous, pockmarked nose. Nibbling on the sandwich, I introduced myself, only to be greeted with a suspicious glare.

'Odd name. I say, you're not German are you?'

Telling him my ancestors were possibly Welsh, I stuffed the sandwich in my mouth and attempted to give him his receipt.

'Oh, don't worry about that. We'll sort that out later. Welsh you say? I went to Wales once. Look here, I'd better get you a drink. Now, don't you move.' He started to walk away, but then stopped. 'I say, have you met Charles? Charles! Keep my delivery chappy friend company will you, while I get him a drink?'

I tried to explain that the order was quite a large one and that I really must be getting on, but Gerald was in top host mood and simply wasn't listening.

'Salt of the earth, old Charles. Top fellow.' Again I tried to get away, but then Gerald dropped the bombshell. 'Charles is in publishing, you know.'

Instantly, my attitude changed. A rush of anticipation overwhelmed me. To an unpublished writer, especially one who drives a van, the word 'publisher' conjures up magical images of awards and respect and paid-off-mortgages.

'Hello,' said Charles, who was rather tall and thin with an odd, mushroom-coloured face.

'Hello,' I said back, not interested in how he looked, only in what he did.

'Could I get you another cucumber sandwich?' he asked, with a broad, child-like smile.

'Yes,' I replied, 'that would be just perfect.' Well, that and a book deal.

'So you drive a van then?'

This comment in isolation told me two things. Charles the publisher had either not been a witness to my auspicious arrival in the rain, or he was simply not a very observant man. Worrying in a potential employer. As I finished off my sandwich and watched the rain bucketing down all around, I warned myself that I might be judging him too harshly.

Telling him that I did, indeed, drive a van, I went on to say that the uniform I was wearing was something I had to bear. 'Every writer struggles at the beginning,' I announced, gravely.

'Oh, you're a writer then?'

Bingo!

That was it. The penny had dropped. I was standing on the threshold of destiny. This was my moment. Over the years, I'd imagined it over and over. And now it was here. I was so nervous. In fact, I was visibly shaking, which was duly noted by Charles. He *was* observant! Oh, joy of joys!

'I think we'd better get you out of those wet clothes, young man. You're going to catch your death. Gerald? Do you have a change of clothing for this young driver chappy?'

I tried to explain I was okay and that the physical reaction stemmed more from excitement than cold, but I didn't get a chance. In seconds, Gerald was back with a huge rug.

'Come on young man, let's have 'em off. Come on, look sharpish – we're all going over to the house now for some food and you don't want to be left here.'

Realising my chance was slipping from me, I slowly took off my shirt. I knew in that moment I needed to stick close to Charles. This, I told myself, might be my only chance. I became dimly aware of everyone staring at me. Gerald leapt to my defence.

'What's the matter with you lot? Have you never seen a chap undress in a tent before?'

'Not one so handsome,' I heard an elderly lady mutter. She smiled over at me. I smiled back sheepishly. You never know, I thought, she might be in publishing too. They might all be publishers!

'When I was in Borneo,' announced Gerald, 'I used to undress in tents smaller than this. In fact, I once put on a dinner suit in a tent.'

As Gerald listed other feats achieved under canvas, I slipped off my trousers, all the time wondering why he would possibly want to wear a dinner suit in Borneo. In seconds I was wearing nothing more than my underwear, boots and a rug. Surrounded by all these strangers, I felt less than comfortable. I noticed Charles running out of the tent towards the house, holding a small tray over his head to protect himself from the torrential rain. Almost in the same moment I heard thunder and felt a huge smack on my back. It was Gerald. He was beginning to get on my nerves. He smacked me again.

'Top man,' he laughed. 'Look at those muscles! You're a strong one. Must be carrying those groceries all day, what?'

Things were getting increasingly bizarre and I was in danger of forgetting why I was there in the first place. I was no longer ahead of my schedule – I was now running late. I should have been and gone, but I had business to attend to. If it meant a book deal with a leading publisher, I would be more than willing to set fire to my van and never return to the store.

'Come on then, young chap. We've got a pig roast on the go over at the house. I was going to use me other pig. She's just as fat and nearly as smelly, but she's good to the kids. Speak of the devil,' he whispered in my ear as Gloria joined us in our sprint for the house.

As we entered the house, Gerald and Gloria disappeared amongst the guests. The room I found myself in was huge and dominated by a winding mahogany staircase. For a moment I wasn't sure what to do, then, quite suddenly, I was struck on the head. I presumed it was Gerald testing my mettle once again, but I was wrong. Somehow I had been struck by an arrow. Luckily for me, it was the type with a rubber sucker. Pulling it from my forehead with a loud pop, I was greeted by a small child with buckteeth, wearing a Chelsea away strip and war paint.

'You're dead, paleface,' he snarled, before snatching the arrow from me and running off into the crowd.

Staring down at my bare legs, work boots and the rug I was still clenching around my throat, I began to suspect he was right. Maybe, somewhere along the line, I had passed away and this was hell. As if to confirm my suspicions, Gerald reappeared, his face as red as a devil.

'There we go, old chap,' he shouted, giving me a plate of food. 'A few more cucumber sandwiches and a couple of pig rolls too. Sliced 'em meself, you know. Once a soldier, always a soldier, what?'

I was just about to question Gerald on Charles-the-publisher's whereabouts, when I spotted my quarry sitting at the bottom of the stairs, dressed – unless I was suffering from concussion from the arrow attack – as a cowboy.

I made my way over.

'Hi,' I said.

'Oh, hello,' said Charles. 'I'm a cowboy.'

I think I said something about it suiting him, or something equally ridiculous, when all I really wanted to do was ask him to read one of my manuscripts.

'Anything to keep the little fellows happy,' he muttered, indicating his costume. 'You're the delivery chappy, aren't you ... and writer?'

Nodding bashfully, happy that he'd remembered, I joined him on the step. I knew then my moment had come and took it with full vigour.

'And you're the publisher...'

'Publicist,' he replied.

'Publicist?' I repeated, shocked.

'Yes, not publisher. Publicist. Big difference between publisher and publicist. Besides, between you and me, I don't like writers. I have to promote 'em, but I don't like 'em. Idle and alcoholic the lot of them. Nothing personal, you understand,' he said, tapping me in what struck me as rather a familiar manner on my 'rugged' arm.

'But Gerald said you were a publisher.'

'Gerald said?' He laughed. 'I'm surprised he knew I did anything!'

Just then a blood-curdling cry prompted Charles to jump to his feet. I looked back to see a group of children at the top of the staircase, all armed with bows and arrows.

'You'll never take me alive, you savages!' cried Charles, unholstering his rather tiny silver gun and running off through the crowd.

Frozen to the spot with disappointment, I found myself suddenly overrun by tiny Native Americans. Then I was alone and I wanted to be anywhere in the world but at the bottom of that staircase, wearing a rug.

Finding an empty armchair on the far side of the room, I ate my food and studied the people all around me. I think I sat there for over an hour. I didn't move. I just watched and thought. It was like a dream. Then I noticed Gloria waving to me with a cheery smile. Her warmth filled me with shame. Being a council estate kid from the north I have spent most of my life despising these wealthy types. Under normal circumstances I would never had ventured into their lives, but because of the rain they had welcomed me with open arms. They were kind, generous people, yet all I had wanted to do was exploit the situation to my own selfish ends.

'Hello,' said Gloria, now at my side. She was in her sixties, pear-shaped, with a pretty face and rosy glowing cheeks. 'Are you all right?'

The words came to me as if in a dream and all I could do was smile and nod. Then I saw my clothes folded in her arms.

'They're dry now,' she said. 'I say, do you have any cream?'

'I'm sorry?'

'Cream ... on your van? We're about to do the strawberries.'

The Van. The delivery. In the space of an hour I had forgotten it all. I had entered another world, where I had briefly imagined a better future. But no...

'Are you sure you are all right?' she asked, and I could see in her eyes that Gloria was a woman who understood life well. With a smile she pulled me to my feet, then averted her eyes as I dressed.

Within minutes I was back at the van. The rain had stopped and the sun was breaking through the cloud. Ahead of me, across the gravel drive, up the steps and through the huge living-room, beneath the winding staircase and into the kitchen, Gloria and Gerald had formed their guests into a human chain, and no sooner had I started to unload the van than it was empty. With a heavy heart, I climbed aboard and started up the engine. As I pulled away, I was aware of the crowd assembled on the drive waving goodbye, but unfortunately less

conscious of the collection of arrows stuck to the back of the van as I drove into the sunset.

Writing's a funny thing. You make up these characters and put them down on paper and you think that's it. But it isn't. From that moment on, they exist. They live, they breathe. Even if you personally never go back to that particular story ever again, somebody else will at some point, and then the characters will live inside them. Oddly enough whenever I'm in Bicester I think of Gerald and Gloria. I imagine them at home and wonder if Charles the publicist has called round for tea.

After coming up with this story I realised I didn't have to write about horrible people. I knew then there was no limit to what I could come up with.

9

The Private Army of Lillingstone Lovell

After a few months in the job I began to get friendly with some of the regulars. One bloke I got to know quite well was a retired soldier. He's a great guy. One weekend he had his children and grandchildren round and as he took the shopping in, one of the kids asked if he would play soldiers with them. I could see from the twinkle in his eye he was more than willing. The next story stems from that moment.

*　　*　　*　　*

Like a lot of men in their forties, I know a thing or two about the Second World War. Names like Dunkirk, Arnhem and El Alamein bring a lump to my throat. So, imagine my surprise on Sunday when I made my way to an address in Lillingstone Lovell called D-Day House. Having never delivered there before, I took the advice of a fellow driver.

'Keep your head down.' He said this with a wry smile. 'Just keep your head down.'

It was just after lunch as I turned onto a narrow track called Normandy Lane. The day was very warm – so much so, I had the window open. It was just a very ordinary day. Or so I thought.

As I manoeuvred the van along the tree-lined lane, I noticed two bushes ahead of me, seemingly blocking the way. Pulling up, I jumped out to take a closer look.

I'd got no more than a couple of metres ... when they moved. I thought this odd. It took me a few moments before I realised that they weren't bushes at all, but two camouflaged children. With guns. Rifles to be precise. More worryingly, they were pointed at me.

Thoroughly startled, I stared back at them. The taller of the two was a girl with long curly hair, around the age of nine or ten, whereas the other, a boy, seemed a little younger. It was difficult to be precise due to their faces being camouflaged with brown and green paint. Dressed in combats and with an assortment of twigs and branches sticking out of their jackets, I had to agree that it was an impressive ambush.

'Password?' said a voice to my right.

Looking in the direction of the voice, I was alarmed to see yet another child appear from the shadows of the wood. Again, firearms were involved, but this one seemed more concerned with the clipboard in his hand. He could have been no more than nine.

'Password?' he repeated.

'I don't know what you mean,' I responded nervously.

'You can't go any further until you give me today's password.'

'I don't know anything about passwords. I've got a delivery for you.'

'A what?' he said, fixing me with a glare.

'A delivery…'

'Well done, that's the password. Please carry on along the lane and watch your speed. Let him through!'

On that, he gave me a brisk salute and disappeared into the trees. I returned to the van. By the time I had started up the engine the road was clear.

As I drove on I was aware of noises and activity ahead. Every now and then I would see a small figure leap from a bush or slit trench, then disappear as quickly as it had appeared. As I got closer, I realised the noises were those of mortar fire and machine gun. Now I was getting worried. Had World War Three begun while I was busy at work?

Before the house was a lawn ... and a tank. Well, I say a tank; it was actually an old van with a dozen or so tyres on either side, and a long pipe sticking out of its non-existent windscreen. Happy it wasn't pointing at me, I carried on to the house.

Throughout my approach, I had been aware of mini-soldiers running to and fro, the air filled with explosions, whistling bullets and death-defying screams. Yet, as I parked up beneath a worryingly low power cable and jumped out, all became silent.

For a moment or two, anyway.

Suddenly, I heard a whizzing sound. Presuming I had inadvertently touched the power cable with the van, I fell to the ground to avoid the resulting electric shock. Instead of a flash, though, I heard someone land by my side. I opened my eyes to see a pair of highly polished boots. There, in an officer's uniform, was another soldier (this one fully grown) staring down at me, disapprovingly.

'My God! Is this the best England can produce? On your feet, man!'

There was another whizzing noise and I looked up to see the child I had spoken to earlier rushing towards me from above. It wasn't a power cable at all, but a zip wire. In a single motion the child flicked his legs forward and released his grip on the pulley. He landed like Olga Korbut. Without a word, the two soldiers saluted one another.

I was now getting very confused.

'Did he know the password?' said the officer.

'Yes, sir.'

'Any chances of him being a spy?'

'I have no reason to suspect that, Grandad – I mean, sir.'

'Okay, Sergeant. Prepare the men.' Turning smartly, the man eyed me up and down and offered his hand. 'The name's Cocksdon-Smythe.'

I bet it is, I thought to myself.

As I introduced myself, I couldn't help but think what an impressive figure Cocksdon-Smythe made. If the wrinkles were any indication, he must have been in his sixties, but his physique was formidable. He was every bit the career soldier. Lean body, short cropped hair, pencil-thin moustache and not a hint of emotion on his shiny shaved face.

'Never seen you before,' he said after a moment. 'No matter. I take it you are fully versed on this week's proceedings?'

'Proceedings?'

'My God, man – is there no communication at your HQ? Were you not told about this week's manoeuvres?' I shook my head. 'Come on then, I'd better give you the tour.'

As we walked I realised the explosions weren't real, but were coming from large speakers suspended in the trees all around us. ALL the 'soldiers' appeared to be children – a dozen or so at least.

'Are they Scouts?' I asked.

'I beg your pardon?'

'The kids. Are they Scouts and Brownies?'

'BROWNIES? SCOUTS? HOW DARE YOU! This is the Glorious Fifth! The finest infantry in the British Army. Brownies indeed...'

Somewhat dismayed, I attempted to give him the grocery invoice.

'Oh, plenty of time for that. No ... you see, twice a year, we have manoeuvres to keep the kids – I mean, the men – on their toes. You never know when we might be called upon.'

As he talked, I heard a vehicle behind me, but I was so engrossed in what he had to say, I didn't bother to look round.

'And what's today's exercise?' I asked.

'Today, red team will attempt to prise back essential supplies taken by the enemy, who today will be represented by blue team.'

'And how will this be done?' I asked, as the sound of the vehicle became louder.

'Well, it's very simple. Blue team will be given ten minutes to take away the vehicle in question and prepare defences. Red team will then have exactly half an hour to try and get it back.'

Something was stirring in my mind ... it was that odd feeling we all have just before the penny drops.

'Vehicle?'

'Vehicle.'

No sooner had the word left his lips than I heard a beep from an oncoming vehicle. My vehicle. It was being driven – unless I was very much mistaken – by the curly-haired, camouflaged girl I had met in the lane, sticking out her tongue as she went by.

'You can't do that!' I protested as the van passed us. 'That's company property!'

Like the head of a viper, his finger shot to the end of my nose. It was an odd moment. I've never been threatened by a finger before.

'Get a hold of yourself, man.' His voice was steady, but firm. 'Company property? Company property! My God, you should be ashamed of yourself! Was that what Frost's men said at Arnhem when they were outnumbered ten to one – "Now look here, you Germans, could you stop shooting at us, please, these uniforms don't belong to us"?'

'But the van's full of groceries,' I pointed out. 'I've still got five more customers.'

'Would you deny these young children – I mean, these young soldiers – this valuable experience? Are your customers more important than that?'

'Well, frankly, yes!' I shouted. 'I could get in a lot of trouble if I don't make those deliveries, and if anything happens to that van.'

For a moment he just looked at me, his finger still on my nose.

'Sergeant! Put this man on a charge!'

'Oh, for God's sake!'

I'd had enough. They'd stolen my van. This was war.

'Will you get a grip?' I yelled. 'This isn't real – these aren't soldiers! They're children! And I've got to get on!'

No sooner had I finished the sentence, than I was upended. With incredible speed and efficiency, three small children rolled me onto my front and tied my hands behind my back.

'Get off me!' I stormed.

'I wouldn't struggle, man – they're fully-trained Commandos, you know. The SAS survival manual is their favourite bedtime book. They're like sponges at this age,' he added with grandfatherly pride.

I continued to scream and shout, but by then the focus had gone from me to a small wood at the end of the lane.

A battle had begun, in more ways than one.

As I lay on the ground with my hands bound, I began to get incredibly angry. But it wasn't because three small children had overpowered me, or because their grandfather had put them in his fantasy world. No, it was something more. It took me a while to see it, but as I lay on the grass, I realised it was because I was jealous. I was jealous of this disregard for reality.

At what point in my life did I put away my toys? When did I get so boring?

As I watched Cocksdon-Smythe and his private army that afternoon, I realised that it's okay to escape into our fantasy worlds from time to time. Regardless of what you might hear in the media, most of us are good people. Of course, we have our faults but the vast majority of us do not abuse our children, we do not murder on the quiet. Even though we feel isolated sometimes, we all face the same problems. Day after day, we endure our bloody awful jobs, the depressing media and watch from afar as talentless celebrities make more money in a week than we do in a year.

Yes, I think we deserve our little fantasies from time to time.

Somehow I managed loosen my bonds and sit up. As I did so, I felt a great sense of relief. In the space of five minutes I'd become free ... in more ways than one.

Somehow, over the years, I'd become a 'Company Man'. I'd put away my dreams and given up. Inadvertently, Cocksdon-Smythe had shown me a lot about myself.

Slowly I walked in the direction of the wood at the end of the lane. The sound of explosions were once again filling the air. As I entered the wood, I could see my van in a small clearing just ahead. The girl with the curls and the tongue was still in the cab, but now she was throwing water bombs at oncoming troops, who in turn were throwing bags of flour at her. She seemed to be the only member of Blue Team left now but, despite being completely outnumbered, she fought valiantly. It was an inspiring sight.

I spotted her grandfather in a slit trench and made my way over.

'She's got some spirit,' I said, clambering down. 'You must be very proud.'

As Cocksdon-Smythe turned to face me, I think I saw a tear of grandfatherly pride in his eye. By his side sat the remaining members of Blue Team, their dejected faces covered in flour.

'Is she the only one left?' I asked.

'It's just a matter of time now. She's running out of water – I mean, ammunition.'

Just then, as a series of flour bombs splattered against the van's windscreen, a wicked thought entered my mind.

'These manoeuvres,' I said, 'is there any rule that says you can't use reinforcements?'

'I suppose not ... the problem is, I don't have any more troops.'

I smiled broadly and suddenly he seemed to understand.

'You don't mean – you're not suggesting – you wouldn't?'

'I would, you know.'

'You'd help young Tabitha – I mean – that young soldier? Oh, you've made me quite emotional – you're not as bad as I thought. Okay then, you'd better go – she hasn't got long. I'll tell you what – I'll even bend the rules and give you covering fire. Off you go then!'

No sooner had I left the trench than small bags of flour were whizzing past my head. Miraculously, I managed to reach a huge oak on the edge of the clearing without being hit, but there I was pinned down. Every now and then I would hear a small thud against the tree, followed by a cloud of flour. It was already going horribly wrong: I'd lost the element of surprise.

It was then I noticed one of the children who had tied me up. He was sitting in a hollowed-out tree eating a bag of sweets. I decided I would make him pay for his moment of selfishness. Rushing across the clearing, I dived headfirst into the hole. He seemed startled, which of course had been my plan all along.

'Don't move,' I said, picking up a bag of flour by his side. 'What's your name?'

'Bertie...' he muttered, his lower lip quivering with fear.

'Well, Bertie my boy, you're now my prisoner. Where's the rest of your ammunition?'

He pointed to a pile of flour bags beside him and started to cry. I wanted to give him a cuddle, but there's no place for sympathy in the theatre of war. Stuffing the bags into my pockets and taking a handful of sweets from his bag, I stood at the entrance and waved over to his grandfather.

'INCOMING FIRE!' he yelled.

It was the distraction I had hoped for. I ran out like Redford and Newman in *Butch Cassidy and the Sundance Kid*. But there would be no sad ending here – a child's life was at stake. Running amongst Red Team, turning their little camouflaged faces powdery white with extraordinary accuracy, I was a child myself once more. Before I knew it I was at the van, relieving the brave and defiant young Tabitha.

It only lasted a matter of seconds, but my moment of glory will live with me forever.

After a quick inspection of the troops, I was invited back to the house for tea, which, with my prisoner, Bertie, on my shoulders, I accepted gracefully.

I was incredibly late for my remaining customers that afternoon. But I didn't care. Thanks to Cocksdon-Smythe and his private army, I had realised that sometimes life is too short to worry about such things.

10

Boys Will Be Boys

In mid-May of that first year, summer finally arrived in England. The day was Sunday and, as if to celebrate the coming of summer, two small children decided to ambush my van with water bombs.

We get a lot of this. We're an easy target. I think in a lot of cases it's encouraged by their parents. A type of revolt against big business. Personally I don't mind it. In fact, I encourage it.

*   *   *   *

I got ambushed on Sunday. Kids, eh? They're so versatile. In winter it's snowballs; on Bonfire Night, strategically placed rockets; and in summer ... water bombs. What else?

The day was cloudless and very warm, so warm I had the window down. It was lovely. Around two o'clock, I had just made my last delivery in a small close, when I saw these two little ... fellows, hovering near a children's playground just ahead. They were in a huddle, pointing at me. Not a good sign.

What I didn't realise, but they had, was that I had to pass them as I turned the van round. But as I started up the engine and made my way towards them ... they disappeared. Then, out of nowhere, I saw a water balloon cross my vista.

'What the – ?' I exclaimed as the thing landed on the far pavement.

Then came another. Missed. This one went over the van. As I reversed, they tried again, but once more it was nowhere near. Now, however, I found myself offering

them their best target yet – my open window. But I was too good for 'em. Reversing quickly, the next leaky balloon shot harmlessly across my bow. As I completed my turning manoeuvre, they started to run off but, by driving forward, I managed to cut off their escape.

'Oi! You two! Come here!'

'Sorry, mister,' said the first of them.

'Never mind all that,' I told him.

'It was only a bit of fun, Mr Deliveryman,' said the other.

'Am I laughing?'

'No,' they said in unison.

I got out of the van.

'Does your mother know you're out here causing mayhem?'

This enquiry was greeted with quivering lower lips. I then noticed they still had one balloon left.

'You should be ashamed of yourselves. When I was your age, you wouldn't have caught me doing that. You threw four water bombs at that van – and missed every time! You're a disgrace to your generation! This is what comes of playing on Play Station all day. You need to get out more. What you should have done, was wait until I'd stopped to reverse, and then hit me with a flanking movement. Both of you attacking me at the same time, you see. Trust me, lads – it's a lot easier hitting a sitting duck than a speeding one. And the way you're throwing is all wrong. It's all in the wrist action, you see. Give me that balloon.'

Nervously, the elder of the two handed over his weapon.

'Now then,' I said, looking round for a suitable target. 'Do you see that tyre hanging in the playground?'

'The one near the road?'

'Yes, now watch the way I position my feet as I prepare myself. Now putting my left foot forward thus, I give myself extra leverage for distance, allowing my right foot suitable anchorage to maintain my aim. Got all that?'

A shared nod told me they had.

'Now, if I take a step back and move into that position, keeping my wrist firm, but open, it allows me the three elements required of consistent throwing. Accuracy, distance and speed. And the great thing is, you can use this with snowballs, rocks, balls, the lot. Okay, now watch this!'

Now, I don't like to blow my own trumpet, but it was a throw of majestic proportions.

Over the swings, past the roundabout, through the tyre – and through the open window of a passing police car.

'Right, lads, I'm off,' I told them rapidly as I handed them a pound each. 'When the policeman comes over, whatever you do, don't tell him it was me.'

'For another pound,' said the eldest boy, 'we won't tell them who you work for either.'

11

Marriage Guidance

I don't know if you've ever watched *Father Ted* on TV or not. Kevin McKidd was in it once, you know. Yes, he likes to taunt me with his TV and film appearances. Anyhow, if you have, you must remember the couple who are always arguing – that is, until they see Father Ted. Then they change and become very lovey-dovey. Well, we drivers see a lot of that. Often, we hear couples screaming and shouting at each other as we approach a residence, but then they stop at the sound of the doorbell. It's a lot more common than you may realise.

Looking on the bright side, though, it's great material for a funny story.

* * * *

One day, whilst serving the fine people of Buckinghamshire, I was knocked out. It's true. A full-blown-darkness-descending-body-on-the-ground-stars-spinning-around-my-head-knock-out. But this moment didn't arise from a fall ... neither did it come from the fist of an irate housewife. No, it was much stranger than that. But by now I'm sure you will have come to expect nothing less.

It was a Sunday and I was in Bicester (again). I knew where I was going and I knew what to expect: Mr and Mrs A of Winton Close are legendary amongst us delivery drivers.

Even before I'd turned off the engine I could hear them. How sad it is to hear a couple fight ... especially when you're about to speak to them.

Comments like 'You !*?!!*' And 'Shut up, you stupi *!*?!' were filling the air as I jumped out of the cab and begin to unload. 'Crash!' went a pot. 'Bang!' went ... something not as fragile as a pot. I glanced around at the other houses. 'How do they put up with it all day?' I asked myself. I find it hard enough during the five-minute delivery once a week.

I have a confession to make here. I don't like Mr an Mrs A. I don't even have any sympathy for them. I'm on thankful they don't have any children. And the reason I don't like them? Read on.

I braced myself against the torrent of hatred and approached the door. Placing the groceries on the ground and a finger on the doorbell, I smiled to myself. You see, I knew in that moment that what I was about t do would turn me into a God. With one tiny movement, would bring peace to Bicester.

Ding Dong!

Instantly, silence descended on the house. I heard scurrying sounds and saw hurried movement through the coloured glass of the front door. Then the door opened to reveal the couple, smiling like young lovers.

'Oh, hello!' they said in unison.

'Hello,' I answered, when all I really wanted to do was bang their heads together.

'What a lovely day,' said Mrs A.

'I think we're in for a fine spell,' added Mr A.

This charade, this pantomime, has carried on since I began. During my brief acting career I experienced plenty of pantomime, but on this particular Sunday the pantomime turned sour and soon we had a tragedy. On this day they had managed to involve me in their little war of attrition.

With the delivery complete, I started up the engine and began to pull away. Then I realised I'd forgotten their frozen food. It's a common occurrence with me. So out I got to deliver the single tray. As I approached the door, I realised it was slightly ajar. Pushing it open, I placed the tray on the floor and looked up. Big mistake.

In the same moment I heard a yell and saw a flash of silver moving towards me at great speed.

Smack!

I felt intense pain across my forehead. Something had hit me. Correction – something hard had hit me. Something tin-shaped. Something tin-shaped with beans and sausages on the label. In seconds, I was falling into an abyss ... darkness was descending from all around. In short, I had been knocked out.

All I remember after that was being aboard a sausage-shaped ship called Heinz on a vast sea of beans in a rich tomato sauce. I only hoped the injury wouldn't leave any lasting damage. I've got enough as it is.

When I woke a little later, not only did I have the mother of all headaches, but I realised I was in a different place. Happy that I wasn't dead and that this wasn't apparently a 'better place', I tried to surmise my location.

Now, unless I had indeed sailed on the good ship Heinz through the hall, dining room and kitchen, someone had carried me from the front door, onto the patio and into a hammock. Above me, Mr and Mrs A were in deep conversation. They looked rather worried. And so they should. Attempted murder carries a heavy tariff in this country ... and we don't deliver to prisons.

Even though they were whispering, I could hear every word they were saying (this is Mr and Mrs A we're talking about, don't forget – quiet isn't something they excel in). Unaware that I was awake, they were discussing a recent occurrence in which a delivery driver fell over on a customer's drive and attempted to sue the said customer. I was aware of the case, as were my concerned employers.

As I watched the couple debating this and relating it to their own rather unique problem, a wicked thought entered my mind. Then I saw Mrs A looking down at me.

'Oh, you're awake,' she said. 'How are you feeling? I'm afraid you've had quite a bang on the head ... you see, you fell over.'

I fell over?

'You tripped up,' added her husband.

I tripped up? His smile was as smug as that of a double-glazing salesman.

'Yes,' Mrs A muttered. 'You tripped up on the pavement next to your van. Outside our property.'

'That's right,' continued Mr A. 'You fell over on the pavement ... next to your van. OUTSIDE our property.'

I don't think I have ever seen barefaced lying on that level before. It was extraordinary. Maybe they were politicians?

'How are you feeling?' asked Mrs A, mopping my brow.

I sat up.

'I'll tell you how I'm feeling. Disappointed. Disappointed that two grown people who seem to spend their days screaming at each other can only find harmony in adversity!'

Okay, it was a bit melodramatic, but then I wasn't in the best of moods.

'I don't know what you mean,' said Mr A, outraged.

'Yes, you do.'

'How dare you!' he continued.

Oddly, I didn't feel an ounce of remorse or worry for what I'd said. This was a unique situation. I had the upper hand. I could say what I liked. I mean, what could they do? They'd very nearly taken my head off. I was suddenly filled with a wonderful sense of power. Litigation is an ugly word to me – I wouldn't dream of suing my fellow man, but they didn't know that.

'I'd like a cup of tea. Milk, two sugars,' I informed them.

'What?' replied Mr A.

'Tea,' I said. 'Earl Grey – I know you've got it. It was in the second tray.'

'How dare you – ow!' Mr A yelped as his wife kicked him in the shin.

'Frank, shut up!' she scowled, before returning to my fevered brow. 'Would you like a biscuit as well?'

'That would be lovely ... maybe one of those nice chocolate bourbons I just delivered?'

'Of course,' she said, hurrying inside.

I lay my head back on the hammock and slowly begin to sway in the sun, eyes closed. I heard Mr A starting towards the house after his wife.

'Oh, Frank?'

'Er ... yes?'

'Be a love and ring my manager would you? Explain I'm injured and can't continue?'

'What?'

'I think it's important that she realises that I've had a bang on the head. Just tell her you're looking after me for a while. Tell her I'll drive back in an hour or so.'

'Uh?'

I opened my eyes and looked directly at him. 'And you might want to mention that my fall was on the pavement ... OUTSIDE your property?' I added, with a little wink.

'Oh, I see,' he muttered, a smile appearing on his face. 'Yes, yes, of course. No problem. Have you got the number?'

'I would have thought it was in the yellow pages, Frank. Oh, and Frank, have you got the Sunday paper?'

And so, an hour later, assisted by my new friends, I walked slowly to the front door.

'Can we say we'll hear no more about this unfortunate incident?' Frank enquired nervously as I walked out.

I turned slowly. 'On one condition. That you two make the effort to get on. Or, failing that, learn to argue and throw things in a quieter fashion. Is that possible, do you think? I mean, even if you don't want to do it for yourselves, think of your neighbours. And my head.'

In a loving embrace, they promised they would try their best, and on that positive note I got back in my van. Before I could drive off, however, I heard a tap on the window. It was Mrs A.

'Sorry,' she said, with an apologetic smile, 'but in all the chaos I realised I wanted to send something back.'

'Not a problem,' I muttered, reaching for a pen, 'what is it?'

'It's this tin of beans and sausages ... it's all dented.'

I don't know if the neighbours heard the scream from the man in the van, but if they had, I'm sure it would have been water off a duck's back.

12

Rear Window

One day during that summer, I delivered to a very odd man who was convinced his neighbour was pinching pegs off his washing line. No, really. I didn't say anything, but I found it hilarious. Later that night I watched an Alfred Hitchcock film. When I woke next morning I found, subliminally, my mind had been busy

*　　*　　*　　*

I had a very bizarre experience on Sunday. I was over in a village called Fritwell, with only two deliveries to go. Those final two deliveries were FTDs (First Time Deliveries.)

Happily for me, both of the deliveries were within a street of each other. Great, I thought, this shouldn't take me too long. But, as you will already know, life never works out like that for me.

On the door of the first house was a note telling me to take the groceries through to the kitchen. I did as instructed, aware that there was someone in the dining room. Having emptied the trays onto the table, I knocked on the door.

'Come in,' said a male voice, almost in a whisper.

The room was in almost complete darkness. This was odd, mainly because it was only two o'clock in the afternoon. For some reason, an armchair had been pushed up to the window and the curtains drawn around it, allowing the occupant to peer out into the garden.

I moved closer.

'Hi. I've put your groceries in the kitchen. I just need a signature.'

'Shhhhhh!' said the shape. 'Be quiet and come here.'
'What's up?' I asked.
'Here – take a look.'

As the man turned to me, a small shaft of sunlight pierced the darkened room. I could just make out the form of a skinny man in his late sixties, with a short stubbly beard, holding a pair of binoculars. As I took them from him, he moved from the chair so I could get a better view.

'What am I looking at?' I enquired.

'Shhhhh! Keep your voice down. Do you see the man in the garden at the bottom of the hill?'

'Yes.'

'Do you know him?'

'No. Should I?'

'Everybody will soon.'

'Why?'

'We'll come to that. What's he doing now?'

'He's cutting the grass.'

'Don't you find that odd?' he asked.

'Not in the middle of summer, no. Here – why are we whispering?'

'I don't want him to overhear our conversation.'

'He's about two hundred feet away.'

'Yes, but he's a crafty one. I've been watching him for a while.'

'Why?'

'We'll come to that. Now, what would you say if I told you he cut the grass yesterday as well? And that he cuts the grass two or three times every week.'

'Yes, I suppose that is a bit odd.'

'Look over to the left. Do you see that mound of soil?'

'Yes.'

'What do you think that's for?'

'I don't know … maybe he's about to plant something there?'

'Oh, he's planted something there, all right. His wife.'

'His wife!'

'Shhhhhh!'

'His wife?' I repeated, in a whisper.

'They are always arguing. It's terrible. One night, about two weeks ago, it was so bad I looked out to see him and his wife having a real ding dong in the bedroom.'

'I see.'

'No, not like that!' he snapped, scowling. 'An argument. She was screaming. It was terrible. A horrible gurgling sound.'

'Everybody argues from time to time.'

'Yes, they do. But them two won't again ... because ever since that night there's been no sign of her.'

'Maybe she's gone on holiday?'

'That's what he wants us all to think. But I've been watching him. Four days later, the dining room curtains were closed and that mound of soil appeared. Now, what do you think about that?'

'Have you rung the police?'

'Not yet. Not until I've got a watertight case. That's why I've locked myself away in this room. That's why I've started having my food delivered. I'm gonna get the bugger, if only for the memory of that poor woman.'

'Look, I'd better be going. Could I get a signature?'

As he signed, he looked up at me. 'You have to promise me something. If you can't get an answer next time you come, go to the police. Don't hesitate, because he's a crafty one and I have a feeling he's onto me.'

Promising him I would, I went back to the van. I have to admit I was spooked by the whole affair. Happy that I only had one more delivery, I drove round the corner to a street parallel to the one I had just been to. To a house opposite the house I had just delivered to. Yes, you guessed it. I was delivering to the house of the potential wife murderer.

It could only happen to me.

As I approached the house, I saw a note telling me to take the groceries through to the kitchen. As I had done at the previous address, I did as instructed. Once inside, I could see through the kitchen window, and hear from the occasional shuffle or thud from within the house, that the grass cutter had finished and was now in the dining room. I could also see the mound of soil. It was a macabre sight, but I didn't let it put me off. I owed it to the man's late wife to uncover some telltale sign of murder. Were there any splashes of blood across the ceiling? No, there were not. A limb in the bin? Again, no. It was a frustrating five minutes.

When I'd finished my search and unpacked, I knocked on the dining room door.

'Come in,' said a male voice, almost in a whisper.

The room was in almost complete darkness. A sense of déjà vu washed over me. In that moment, everything I'd heard at the previous house echoed in my head. 'She was making a terrible gurgling sound ... she hasn't been seen since ... I think she's buried in the garden.'

Simply put, I was terrified. What if he wasn't *just* a wife murderer? What if he enjoyed his work? What if he saw me as a potential victim?

'Come over here,' said the voice.

By this time, my eyes were getting quite used to darkened rooms. I looked over to see that the set-up was similar to the previous house. Again, there was an armchair pushed up to the window, with the curtains drawn around it. Although this man was rather fat, he had adopted the same stance and was peering out into the garden. Shaking like a leaf, I joined him over by the window.

'Er ... I've put your groceries in the kitchen. I just need a signature.'

'Shhhhhh!' said the fat man. 'Be quiet and come here.'

'Hey?' I said nervously.

'Come here! Here – take a look.'

As the man turned to me, a small shaft of sunlight pierced the darkened room. I could see he hadn't shaved for days.

'Here,' he said, passing me the binoculars, 'take a look.'

I took them from him and sat down in the chair. Unlike the other man, this one had devised a box with a piece of mesh across the front. I looked through it. Although it affected the view a little, I could clearly see my friend at the top of the hill looking down at us.

'What am I looking at?' I muttered awkwardly.

'Shhhhh! Keep your voice down. Do you see the house at the top of the hill? The one with the curtains closed?'

'Yes.'

'Who do you think is in there?'

'I dunno,' I said innocently. 'Jimmy Stewart?'

'What? No! That, my friend, is a thief.'

'How do you mean?'

'We'll come to that. Can you see the binoculars?'

'Yes.'

'Ah ha!' He laughed. 'We can see him, but thanks to my clever filtering set-up, he can't see us!'

By this time my nerves were distinctly on edge. I simply didn't know what to do next.

'He's a crafty one. I've been watching him for a while. But I'm craftier. He's not the first man to try and discover my secrets.'

'Secrets?' I said, my voice quivering to the highest of octaves.

'Yes, for the last ten years my marrows have won prize after prize round here. And I've worked bloody hard to get where I am. I'm not letting no thief pinch my secrets. I'll go to any length. There they are, over there, just behind that mound of soil. I put that there to keep them out of sight of that nosy bugger!'

It all began to make sense. But what about his wife?

'Does your wife not mind you spending so much time on your vegetables?' I asked, tentatively.

'A marrow is not a vegetable, young man. It is a fruit,' he growled. 'No, the wife hates it. But I love my garden, love being out there with nature.'

'Your lawn looks nice.'

'Oh yes, I'm very proud of my lawn. I spend a great deal of time on that, you know.'

'Yes, I've heard – I mean, yes, I can see.'

'Not that the wife appreciates it. But she's got her opera, so each to their own.'

'Opera?'

'Yes, she sings with the local operatic society.'

'Oh. Is she any good?'

'Bloody awful. She even has me helping her out sometimes. They're doing that *Sweeney Todd* at the moment and she has me doing all the actions to help her rehearse. It's a horrible experience. It's a brave man who can stand within six foot of her when she's got her mouth open. The sounds she makes when she sings! It's like a throttled cat.'

'Is she out today?'

'She's at her sister's for a fortnight. That's why I decided to have my groceries delivered. I hate shopping.'

Now it all made sense. Suddenly the phone rang.

'Oh bugger! What time is it?' he asked, putting the light on.

'Ten past two. Why?'

'That'll be her. I should have picked her up from the station at two. Answer it for me, would you? Tell her I'm on my way.'

As he ran out I picked up the phone. 'Hello?'

'Frank, where the bloody hell are you?' screamed a female voice.

'Sorry – I'm a deliveryman. Your husband's just left to pick you up.'

'I'll bloody kill him,' she said. 'Hang on, I don't have home delivery.'

'You do now.'

'Oh, what a day! I'm sure I'm going to die, you know,' she added.

I nearly dropped the phone. 'What did you say?'

'I said I think I'm going to die. There were no drinks on the train. I haven't had a cup of tea since Crewe. My throat's like the bottom of a bird's cage.'

'Yes,' I replied, with a smile. 'So I've heard.'

13

Witch

In that first year I was happier than I had been in a long time, but as autumn approached and the rejections from publishers and literary agents mounted, I began to get down again. What if all my writing came to nothing? How would I feel if I was never published and was to retire at seventy as a van driver? I could almost see an image of a tired, white-haired, old man, struggling to make the deliveries on time. 'That's 'Old Lee',' the younger ones would say. 'Rumour has it he was once in *Coronation Street*, but went mad through lack of work. Ever since then he's been driving a delivery van. Don't look into his eyes for too long, though. The emptiness will overwhelm you.'

The more down I became, the less keen I was to write funny stories. So much so I started to write darker ones.

*   *   *   *

One of the most beneficial things about being a delivery driver is discovering unique architecture tucked away on private roads. Not that I'm a snob, you understand, or that I truly appreciate the variety of architectural styles, but, as somebody once put it, I know what I like.

A while ago, while delivering to a farm near Poundon, a small village on the way to Bicester, I noticed an old, dilapidated house in the distance. There was something about the place that caught my eye. I even mentioned it to the farmer during the delivery.

'That?' he said, watching me as I emptied the van. 'That's Raven House ... just hope you don't have to deliver there, young fella.'

'Why's that?'

'Because that's where Old Lizzie lives...'

'Old Lizzie?' I muttered, my interest growing by the second.

'Old Lizzie Baxter,' he said, teasingly, 'the Poundon Witch.'

'Take no notice of him, dear,' said his wife, appearing from the farm, 'she's not a witch at all. She's just a frail old lady, keeps herself to herself. Rumour has it she used to be an actress and retired after her fiancé died tragically. Occasionally we see her sister calling to check on her.'

As I left the farm, I couldn't help but stare at the house in the distance. Now I saw it in a different light. Now it had a darker quality. As the road veered off towards Twyford, I briefly saw the whole of the house through a gap in the trees. It was only a second or so, but it was clear that it had once been a grand house. Not anymore. Now it was falling apart, a roost for crows, rooks and, dare I say it, ravens.

I don't know why this experience stayed in my head. Maybe it was because of the farmer's comments. I mean, how often do you hear the word 'witch' in everyday conversation? Maybe it wasn't that at all - maybe it was the reference to the 'theatre'? I was once an actor, don't forget, and we theatrical types tend to have a bond that remains long after the curtain has dropped.

Then, last weekend, I had reason to recall it all again.

Before each run, we delivery drivers like to check where we're going. I had eleven deliveries that day – nine in Bicester, one in Launton and the final one on the outskirts of Poundon. This delivery had a little star next to it indicating a 'new customer'. I didn't really think much of it until I saw the surname, Baxter. Miss Elizabeth Baxter.

In that moment, the farmer's comments came back to me like a wave. 'That's where old Lizzie Baxter lives, the Poundon Witch.'

It didn't really spook me that much. Well, not at first. The thing was, having seen the dilapidated Raven

House, I was not what you might call 'keen' on making a delivery there.

All through that Sunday my apprehension grew stronger as I got closer and closer to the final delivery. Before I knew it, I was leaving Launton on the Twyford road for Poundon, for Raven House and Lizzie Baxter.

Near Poundon I passed the narrow lane that led to the farm I'd visited a few months earlier. After a minute or so more I saw another lane off to my right, this one even narrower thanks to a long, suffocating wall of hawthorn and privet. Somehow I managed to squeeze the van onto the lane until I saw an opening ahead. As I steered the van beneath the branches of a huge oak, I saw Raven House up close for the first time.

It was as if I'd entered a Hammer horror set.

Even though the roof had collapsed on one side and the remaining beams stuck out like bones through skin, the house was an impressive sight. I turned onto a gravel drive, now partially overgrown with nettles and grass, and found space to park beside a redundant fountain across from the main entrance. As I got out I became aware of dozens of crows, rooks and ravens staring down at me from the broken roof. I slammed the door. With a deafening cawing and screeching, they flew above the house, briefly darkening the sky. Then all was silent once more. Even though there was a busy road only a mile or so away, the trees and bushes soundproofed the house from the outside world.

I climbed the steps and knocked on the huge black door. Nothing. I knocked again and again. The place seemed deserted.

Deciding Miss Baxter might be casting a few spells round the rear somewhere, I walked round, past the dilapidated part of the house. As I did so, I was surprised to find a small garden, with neat rows of vegetables and a small orchard. Suddenly I heard a crackling noise. I glanced over to see a small bonfire at the bottom of the garden with a narrow thread of smoke escaping towards the sky.

Reassured that there appeared to be no cauldron suspended above the fire, I made my way towards the house. The back door was open.

'Hello, Miss Baxter,' I called nervously into the interior. Nothing. 'Hello? I have a delivery for you.'

Again, nothing.

Taking a few steps back, I glanced up. A chill ran through me. Someone was watching me from an upstairs window. Due to the dirt on the pane I couldn't see who (or what) it was. I waved but almost instantly the shape backed into the shadows. Presuming it was Lizzie on her way down, I waited. All in vain. Five minutes later, there was still no response. Then I heard the sound of a voice.

'Hello?' I called again. 'Miss Baxter?'

I heard the voice again. Was it directed at me? The farmer's wife did say she was frail. Was Lizzie confined to her room maybe? I decided to go in.

Ahead of me was a long darkened hallway. It wasn't until I was halfway down it, though, that I realised the walls were covered with photographs. Using a small torch – I used to be in the scouts – I studied the lines of black and white images. Most of them were of the theatre, and in each one there was a beautiful young lady with long dark hair. I knew it was Lizzie.

As I reached the far end of the hall, I came across a small group of pictures of Lizzie with a man. Her fiancé? I recalled what the farmer's wife had said. 'He died, tragically.'

Then I heard the voice once more. It was louder now, loud enough for me to realise the words were not being spoken at all, but sung. The sound was faint, a haunting whisper. Somehow I knew it was Lizzie. I hadn't even seen her, but already there was a feeling I knew her well. It's funny, but I didn't want to go without meeting her, witch or no witch.

I groped my way through a large, shadow-filled study and found myself at the foot of a staircase. Was she still upstairs? There was only one way of finding out. I started to climb. Then I heard the voice once more.

It was closer now, easier to define – almost a murmur, in a way, but from it I could somehow sense strength and, dare I say it, authority?

As I reached the top of the stairs I sensed rather than saw a movement down below in the study. The landing at the top of the staircase was very dark; the curtains were still closed and the autumn sun was struggling against the tattered, dirty cloth. I leaned over the banister and peered into the darkness, but couldn't see a thing. Then the voice came again and I realised the noise wasn't coming from upstairs at all, but from the room below.

Somewhere in the shadows, someone was singing.

'Miss Baxter?'

Slowly I descended the stairs back into the study, but as I did so the sound faded away. Then I spotted her by the window.

'Miss Baxter? I have a delivery.'

It was so dark that, other than for a faint outline, I couldn't see her face. I reached for the curtains.

'Leave them!'

I was so startled I stood frozen to the spot.

'What are you doing in my house?' she said, her voice now strong and clear.

'I couldn't get any reply,' I stammered. 'I came to see if you were okay. I have a delivery for you.'

As I spoke and my eyes became accustomed to the light, I realised she was in a rocking chair, swaying slowly to and fro.

'But I haven't ordered anything. How could you have a delivery for me?'

'Maybe a member of your family ordered something for you?'

'Maybe, maybe. What is your name?'

'Lee.'

'And what do you have for me … Lee?' she said, mockingly.

I must be honest – her tone didn't exactly fill me with confidence.

'I've got your invoice. Here, you can have a look.'

Placing it on her lap, I noticed for the first time that she wasn't looking at me at all. Her gaze was fixed on the window or, should I say, the curtains.

'That will be my interfering sister. She likes to make sure I'm all right, make sure I have everything I need.'

She turned slowly to look up at me. 'Didn't they tell you I was a witch?'

'No.'

'Liar.'

As I saw the faint glimmer of ridicule in her eye, I decided to fight back the only way I knew.

'Well, there was some mention of you spooking local teenagers on your broom.'

To my surprise, she smiled. 'And aren't you afraid I might spook you?'

'No, I was in *Macbeth*. You witches don't hold the same fear anymore.'

She laughed. 'You're an actor?'

'Not anymore. I'm retired, like you. Now I'm a just poor deliveryman. Speaking of which, where would you like your groceries?'

No sooner had I finished the sentence than she was singing faintly once more.

'Miss Baxter?' I knelt by her side, but her focus had gone from me back to the window. 'Miss Baxter?'

'You won't get anything out of her now for a while, I'm afraid,' said a female voice from across the room.

I jumped to my feet with fright. I was so startled I didn't know what to say.

'You did well to get what you did. You don't recognise me?'

Recognise her? I could barely see her. Whoever she was, she had bloody good eyesight.

'No? Mind you, I only just recognise you. The last time I saw you, you were wearing a rug.'

The lady at the door was none other than Gloria from the Cucumber Sandwich affair from a few months earlier – the day when I thought I'd found a publisher, the day when I was caught in the rain, and, as Gloria correctly recalled, the day when I wore a rug.

I followed Gloria back along the hallway to the garden, glancing at the many photos adorning the walls as I went. It seemed inconceivable that the beautiful young woman smiling back at me could be related in any way to the frail old woman I had just met. It made me angry that she'd been allowed to fade away like that in this lonely place.

When we reached the garden, Gloria turned to face me. For a moment she just looked at me. Then, as she had done on our first meeting, she read my thoughts.

'Believe it or not, this is what she wants.'

I tried to hide my anger, but it was impossible. 'I do find that hard to believe.'

With a faint smile she turned and walked over to study the dying embers of the fire at the bottom of the garden. I followed her.

'How long has she been here?' I asked.

'Nearly twenty years now. Don't judge me too harshly. I know how it looks. But you don't realise what it's been like for her.'

'I know about her fiancé. How he died tragically.'

Gloria's gentle expression suddenly gave way to anger.

'The only tragic part is that he didn't die sooner. Lizzie was a talented actress and was doing very well until she met him. He was a playwright. They met during a performance of one of his plays in the West End. Before long they were engaged. But as Lizzie's career took off, his failed dismally. He was weak ... jealous of her success. Before long he was drinking and using her as a punch bag. Then, after a particularly heavy night, he choked to death on his own vomit. Not what you might call a very poetic end.'

Taken aback by her sudden outburst, I tried to change tack.

'Did she never go back to the stage?'

'She blamed herself. You see, he had led her to believe his failure was somehow down to her. She was broken. After that the only place she really wanted to be was here, at the place of her birth. At first, she was contented but over the past twenty years she has slowly drifted from me. She used to visit us regularly, but now I can't even get her out of the house.'

'I'm sorry, I didn't realise.'

'It's not your fault,' she said warmly, before adding, 'I think she likes you, though.'

Just then a group of crows descended onto the wooden beams of the broken roof. I looked up and watched as they jostled for space.

'Don't worry. The house is quite secure. Last year she had to spend a few weeks in hospital, so I took the opportunity of having that end of the house bricked up. She has everything she needs. You don't have to worry.' She paused. 'But maybe there is something you could do for her.'

'I'd do anything to help.'

'Her eyesight is not good. I'm sure she would enjoy the company of a young man. One who would enjoy reading to her. A fellow actor, perhaps.'

'I'd be honoured,' I told her.

So there it was. During that brief time I had lived another life, that of Lizzie Baxter, the actress who disappeared all those years ago, the woman now known to all as the Poundon Witch.

14

Home Alone

Before I knew it Christmas had been and gone, and with the dreary winter weather my mood darkened further. The depression was fuelled by many things, the constant rejections from publishers, my position in life as a glorified housewife, and by some of the grumpier customers. One wet Wednesday night at the end of February, I was delivering to a block of flats. Having climbed six flights of stairs (there was a couple shagging in the lift), I was rather peeved to discover there was no one at the address in question, bar a ten-year-old boy. It was a wasted journey. To complete a delivery we require the signature of an adult.

* * * *

'Is your mum or dad in?'

'No.'

'Is there anyone eighteen or over in the house?'

'No.'

'Do you know when your mum or dad will be back?'

'No.'

Conversations like these are commonplace. Often, the delivery driver is faced with the impossible dilemma – to deliver or not to deliver. Sometimes the parents may be 'just round the corner', and sometimes a teenager claims to be eighteen, but of course doesn't have any proof. And sometimes the order, consisting wholly of alcohol and tobacco, as been made by the teenager while their parents are in the Algarve.

But this conversation with this particular child was like no other I've experienced since starting the job. The boy, an angry-looking mite of about nine or ten years,

had taken the monosyllabic response to another level. It was the last delivery of the day and I was ahead of myself, all ready to go back to the store, but I am a conscientious sort of deliveryman. Like a World War Two pilot, I was on a mission: it was my responsibility to drop the payload, regardless of the flack.

'Do you think your parents will be long?'

All I got was a shake of the head.

'Are you all right on your own?'

All I got was a nod of the head.

I turned to go.

'I've got an uncle Billy,' the boy said.

It speaks!

'He'll do. Where is he?'

'Parkhurst.'

I gritted my teeth.

'I could call my mum on her mobile.'

'Go on then,' I muttered.

After a short delay, he returned to explain she would be back in fifteen minutes. Taking the lad at his word, I unloaded the small delivery and helped him put it away. Then we sat at the table. He'd stopped talking again but, being the adult, I felt obliged to make the effort.

'What does your mum do?'

'Works at the cinema.'

Cinema? Failed actor or no, I'm always on the lookout for an opportunity to impress. 'I was in a film once.'

'Was you?'

'Yes. Only a short one. It was for a film festival. I played a soldier...'

'Played?'

'Yes ... I was an actor.'

He stared at me, quizzically. 'My dad says actors are poofs.'

'He does, does he?' Deciding not to take this lying down (even though I was sitting down), I leapt to the defence of the only profession I've ever been good at. 'It isn't easy being an actor, you know. It's not all prancing about on stage. It can be a very tough.'

'My dad says all actors are lazy poofs in love with themselves, who are too lazy to do a proper job.'

Even though I had never met his father, I had quickly reached the conclusion I did not like him. How dare he poison this innocent mind with such spurious bile! Realising the child might be under a misapprehension of what an actor was, I decided to fight on.

'Have you seen *Gladiator*?'

'Yes. It's one of my dad's favourite films.'

Now I've got him.

'Well, don't you realise that in that film all Russell Crowe is doing is playing a part? He is simply acting.'

'My dad says Russell Crowe is the biggest poof of all.'

I knew in that moment that it was going to be the longest fifteen minutes of my life.

The kid had got my back up and there was tension in the air, a sort of Mexican stand-off across the table. He was staring at me – but I wasn't taking him on. Instead I looked around the small kitchen.

The sink was piled high with dirty dishes and the windows hadn't been cleaned (inside or out) for quite some time. Even the kitchen table had become a sort of tapestry of encrusted food.

'You couldn't have been very good,' the boy said, with a mocking smile.

'What?'

'At acting. I mean, if you had been any good at it you wouldn't be driving a delivery van, would you?'

The little bugger was a torturer. Each comment was like a hot poker against the skin, bringing back the pain I thought I'd forgot. Had he no heart?

'How many plays were you in?'

'About a dozen.'

'Twelve. Is that a lot for an actor?'

'No.'

The tables were turned. I was now the monosyllabic child.

'No, it doesn't sound a lot. I bet that Russell Crowe has done more than that. And he's a poof. Are you a -'

'Look, how long is your mother going to be? I've got to get on!'

'There's no need to get excited. She said fifteen minutes and we've only had six.'

It was the other nine I was worried about. What was he going to do next? Bring out the anglepoise and electrodes? Once more I tried to avoid his stare, but he was smiling again. It wasn't a good sign.

'Do the other drivers know you're a failed actor?'

No, they didn't, but I had a feeling with this brat around that wasn't going to last.

'Why do different drivers come each week?' the boy continued.

'There are a lot of drivers and a lot of customers. It's just pure luck I delivered here today.'

If he sensed my sarcastic tone, he didn't say.

'Maybe another driver will come next week?' he said with an even bigger smile.

'Maybe,' I muttered.

God help them. I'm lucky, in a way. I'm still relatively young. Some of the older guys do it to prop up their pension. This thought suddenly filled me with terror. This little bugger could bring on a heart attack in the healthiest of men. If he suddenly had access to us all he could devastate the whole team. And imagine how that would affect the roster!

It seemed as if time had come to a stop and the universe had condensed into the tiny space between us. It was clear the child had some sort of power of me. I was using every trick in the book to maintain my deliveryman charm but, for the first time, I had been found wanting. Adults appreciate well the social parameters. There is a silent understanding between us all. I thought children were unaware of this – but it's just what they like us to think.

Phrases like 'Anything nice planned for the weekend?' and 'Looks like we're set for a bit of rain' would do me no good here. I was drifting aimlessly through uncharted waters. I was dealing with a CHILD … and a heartless one at that.

'Any brothers or sisters?' I enquired.

'Nope.'

The little swine. And why was he just staring at me like that? He was turning me into a quivering mess. In my mind, I could see myself screaming aloud and running out. I had visions of the police finding me next morning slavering in a bush, half-mad. My palms were sweaty and my heart was pounding. Panicking, desperate to calm myself down, I changed tack again. Little did I know where my mindless comment would lead us both.

'So what does your dad do?'

It was as if a wave had crashed over him. He seemed to capitulate before me. It was the riposte I was hoping for and for a moment I felt a rush of exhilaration, but even before I could begin to savour my triumph, he spoke again.

'My dad's in Afghanistan,' he muttered, his eyes now fixed gloomily on the filthy table.

'Oh.'

I had a rush all right, but not one of pride. Shame would have been more precise. There was I, trying to win points against a ten-year-old, and there was his father fighting the Taliban on the other side of the planet.

'You must be very proud of him,' I said, embarrassment pressing me like a vice. 'How long has he been out there?'

'Two years, three months, four days and eighteen hours.'

He was still doing it! He was *still* making me feel inferior! Even now, on the thorny subject of the War On Terror. Damn him and his sad eyes!

'Have you got any children?' he asked, abruptly.

'Two boys.'

'Do they mind you working for a supermarket?'

'If they do they haven't mentioned it.'

The comment should have got me angry, but now I was beginning to understand how my little friend ticked. Fighting back the urge to retaliate, I continued to talk and as I did I realised his view of me had changed.

'It's not what you do in life, you know. It's how you are. Your dad's a very brave man. But we can't all be heroes. Some of us have got to look after our families the best way we can. If I have to drive a van to feed my kids, that's fine by me. And you never know, maybe one day your dad might have to drive a van himself to feed you and your mum.'

His sad eyes seemed to brighten and when he spoke again the tone was very different from before.

'He might get a job with you?'

'You never know,' I replied, happy that my little sermon had served its purpose. But, better still, the tension had lifted and I had expended another six minutes.

'How old are your kids?' the kid asked.

'Nine and six.'

'Is their mum with them now?'

'Yes, but they'll be asleep now.'

'My mum lets me stay up as long as I want.'

I said nothing. I felt sympathy for him now.

'Are you always going to drive a van?'

'I hope not. I write books. My dream is to have one published.'

He seemed amazed by this. 'You write books? That must be hard. I've never read a book.'

'You must have read one at school.'

'Oh yes, but only because I had to. I mean, read a book proper on my own.'

'You should give it a go. My eldest boy loves reading. He reads every night in his room.'

'What – instead of watching TV?'

'He doesn't have a TV in his room.'

The kid nearly passed out. I wasn't sure if he saw me as the anti-Christ or simply mad. 'No TV in his room!'

'I encourage him to read instead.'

It occurred me to then, for the first time, that he must have been left alone a lot of the time. I suppose I should have considered contacting Social Services, but this goes on more than you might think.

'So, who looks after you when your mum's working?'

'One of our neighbours keeps an eye on me.' His mind seemed to be elsewhere all of a sudden. 'How many books has your son read?'

'Lots.'

'I've never read a book.'

'Yes, you said.'

'What is he reading at the moment?'

'He is reading a children's version of *Oliver Twist*.'

'What's that?'

'It's a story about an orphan boy ... it was written by a man called Charles Dickens.'

For a moment or two he was silent. 'I've heard of him. I saw a film once about an orphan boy. There was songs in it.'

'That's *Oliver*. Same story.'

All of this was a revelation to him. From a monosyllabic devil, a boy had appeared before me. I doubt if he had had a conversation like this ever before in his life. The poor little bugger was no doubt left alone in front of his Play Station or the TV all day. Rarely would his imagination be given a chance to bloom. In our final few moments together I thought back to my own childhood. How different it was back then. I was so lucky and I didn't even know.

'I like that film. There's a happy ending. But it's just a story.'

As he said it, I sensed there was more sadness in his world than I had realised.

'I might read a book one day, mightn't I? I mean, on my own?'

'I don't see why not ...' I told him.

He was about to say something more when the front door opened. Without saying a word he jumped up and ran to his room. Almost in the same moment his mother walked in. She was barely a child herself.

'Waiting long?'

'Not long,' I said.

'Yes, sorry, I had a busy night, so I went for a drink with my mate.'

I should have said something. Something like 'How could you leave a ten-year-old child alone all night, you selfish cow?' But, of course, these were mere thoughts, shouting in my head. It's not for me to say. I'm the deliveryman. I'm an irrelevance to these people. But even though I sit on the outside, there are certain times, times like these, where I want to shake the apathy out of their stupid heads.

'Your son and I put away the groceries. He's a nice lad.'

'Oh, you've seen him, have you? You're lucky. He spends most of his time in his room. Right, where do I sign?'

As I passed her the pen, I muttered something about it being difficult looking after a boy with her husband away, but to my astonishment she started laughing.

'He told you that?'

It was not a good laugh. It was a loud and uncaring laugh.

'The little sod! He never knew his dad. Neither did I. I was pukin' out of a window at a party at the time. It could have been one of three. I should never touch vodka. I lose all control. You married?'

I made my way out. It was dark now and raining. But it didn't stop me looking back at the flats as I reached the van. Although the boy's room was in darkness, I could still make out a pair of eyes staring down at me. Now I didn't judge him. Now I understood him well.

Fifteen minutes earlier I would have gladly locked him in a cupboard, but as I drove off that night my mind was flirting with the thought of adoption.

15

Parrot Fashion

Despite my gloomy moods I still tried to find the funnier side of life. Looking for a story one day I remembered some advice an experienced colleague once gave me, during my acting years. You may know it. 'Never work with children or animals.' Having experienced the *children* bit in the previous story, I suppose it was inevitable that I would also come up with one about *animals*. Or to be more precise, *birds*.

*   *   *   *

One evening I delivered to a cottage in Helmdon, in Norhtamptonshire. I knew the address and I knew the lady. I'd been delivering to Mrs Broom for a while and, although she was a little shy, she was always polite.

As I knocked on the door I heard a voice I did not recognise. For a moment or two, I wasn't sure if the voice was speaking to me or not. Then I heard the words 'Come' and 'In'. So in I came.

To my surprise, the kitchen was empty. I called out. No reply. Putting the tray of groceries on the kitchen table, I was about to call out again when I caught movement from the corner of my eye. Looking to my left, I was surprised to see a large parrot on a perch. I was even more surprised when it spoke.

'I'm coming! I'm coming!'

I realised then that it wasn't a person I had heard, but the bird. I also realised I had misheard him. Nevertheless, I was very impressed. I went over to take a closer look.

'I'm coming! I'm coming! Yes! Yes! Yes! Give it to me, big boy! Give it to me, big boy!'

I stopped and stared at the bird. What I was hearing was not quite what I was expecting of a parrot.

'Oh, yes! Oh, yes! Just there! Just there! Spank me! Spank me! I've been a naughty girl!'

I took a step back.

'Oh, you're such a big boy! Oh, you're such a big boy! Same time next week? Same time next week?'

It took me a few seconds to grasp what I was hearing. I hardly knew what to think. What was it going to do next? Have a cigarette?

Just then I heard someone descending the stairs and retreated to the kitchen door.

'Oh, hello,' said Mrs Broom. She seemed somewhat puzzled. 'Are you alone?'

'Yes,' I replied.

'But I heard voices.'

'That wasn't me.' She seemed even more puzzled. 'It was your parrot.'

'Don't be silly, dear,' she said. 'He doesn't speak.'

'Oh, yes, he does,' I thought.

'He hasn't uttered a word in seventeen years. I bought him when my husband passed away. He keeps me company during the lonely nights.'

I was beginning to see Mrs Broom in a new light.

'No man in your life then?' I asked.

'Not really. I do have a gentleman friend. He pops round once a week. He's good with his hands and does the occasional odd job around the house,' she said, playing with her hair.

I glanced over at the parrot. It's difficult to tell with a beak, but I'm sure it was smiling.

'Well,' I told her, 'I can assure you your parrot does speak.'

'Are you sure?' she said, walking over to the bird.

'Quite sure.'

'What did he say?'

'What?'

'When he spoke? What words did he come out with?'

Oh God.

'Well, the usual...' I mumbled, my mind racing, 'who's a pretty boy then – that sort of thing.'

'How marvellous!' she exclaimed. 'Maybe it's the change of environment.'

'I'm sorry?'

'The environment. I normally keep him in the bedroom.'

A very odd noise escaped from my mouth – a sort of 'whatever-you-do-don't-let-the-laugh-come-out' sort of sound. I've never been so embarrassed in my life. My body was pulsing with nervous energy. I couldn't think straight.

'Anyhow, must get on,' she continued. 'The friend I mentioned is coming round soon.'

'Is he a big boy? I mean, is he – is he a local man?' I asked.

'He is actually. Why do you ask?'

'No reason...' I muttered, offering her the pen. 'If you'd just like to spank – I mean, sign – there please.'

Mrs Broom gave me an odd look as she took the pen. I didn't meet her eye but instead stared over at my voyeur friend in the corner. Maybe I was going mad, but I was sure he winked at me.

As I went out, an old gentleman appeared through the gloom.

'Oh, good evening,' he said. He was very much like Mrs Broom in lots of ways, slight, shy, with a small, friendly face.

Well, you know the old saying. Birds of a feather...

16

Giy Forks Hell

After a year or so into the job I had built up a large network of regulars. In most cases I was happy to see people again. To see how our 'doorstep' relationship had grown. It's only natural you remember certain aspects of their lives. And it's funny what you do remember: their jobs, little Billy and the painting competition he entered, how the divorce is coming along, or even their dog's lumbago. But by the same token, this also means you have to return to people that put the fear of God in you. The ones with odd habits and odder pastimes. With this is mind it was inevitable I would revisit certain characters from certain stories.

* * * *

On Bonfire Night, I delivered to one Mrs P of Parkhaven Road, Bicester. You may recall Mrs P from the Yorkshire pudding affair. To this day, I still have nightmares about Rabbits and absent-minded old men.

I've been doing this job for a year now and I am getting pretty savvy about certain elements of what I do. For instance, if you find you're scheduled to work on important days like FA Cup Final day or your birthday, book it off. Give yourself a treat. Bonfire Night is another date to add to the list. Unless you enjoy being ambushed by a group of teenagers using rockets like mortars, it's better to have a night at home.

Having said that, I wasn't ambushed on the night in question. Well, not in the conventional sense. You see, when delivering to Mrs P you have to be prepared. She has this ability to draw you in and get you to do things you simply don't want to do. She's a remarkable woman.

I've been studying her for a while now and I have to admit there's something about her. She plays on your kindness until you can't say no.

As I approached the front door of Mrs P's house, I noticed someone sitting on a deck chair in the shadows.

'Evening,' I said.

The figure didn't reply. And there was a very good reason for that. What I'd encountered was a poor representation of that famous, but unsuccessful, terrorist Guy Fawkes. Happy that no one had witnessed my error, I took a closer look. This made me feel even dumber. It was not at all convincing. In fact it was probably the worst Guy Fawkes I have ever seen. He probably looked more like that after he'd been hung, drawn and quartered. Oddly, he had a look of David Gest about him, but let's not go down that road again. Then I saw the sign.

GIY FORKS – GIV GENERATIONALLY

Not that I'm the greatest speller in the world. Telling myself it was the work of kids, I knocked on the door. Now, that *was* a mistake.

'DELIVERYMAN. DELIVERYMAN. DELIVERYMAN!'

The door opened to three very drunk men singing my job title to the tune of 'Stars and Stripes Forever'. It was not what I was expecting. I could do little other than smile as they continued. A couple of times, I glanced down at David Gest for moral support, but he was no use.

When they'd finished, the trio started to laugh uncontrollably. I didn't join in.

'Evening,' I said, plainly. 'Is Mrs P in?'

'MRS P. MRS P. MRS P!'

Why me?

When they'd finished again, the taller of the three took the invoice from me and tossed it on the sideboard.

'MRS P IS IN THE UVVER ROOM WIV THE UVVER WOMEN, MATE!' Like most drunks he was shouting for no reason. 'WE CAN'T HELP YOU. BECAUSE WE'RE GOING DOWN THE PUB!'

'DOWN THE PUB. DOWN THE PUB. DOWN THE PUB!'

Even though the night was filled with explosions, I could still hear them for the whole time it took me to unload the van. It was not a good sound. They made Jedward sound like Pavarotti.

As I was stacking the trays in the hall, I could hear giggling and shouting from the front room. I must admit, it did not fill me with cheer. When I knocked on the door leading to the front room, it all went quiet – well, apart from an odd buzzing noise, that is. I knocked again. Nothing. I decided to go in.

As I opened the door, I was surprised to see a large group of women staring at Mrs P, who had her back to me. I suppose I'd have recognised that hair anywhere, but it was the vibrating Rabbit in her hand that clinched it. On the far wall there was a hand made poster. It read;

AN SUMERS PARRTY – A LET UR AIR DOWN NITE 4 THE GURLS!

And I blamed the poor spelling of Guy Fawkes on the kids!

'And this, ladies, is my biggest seller – the ten-inch Rabbit.'

Suddenly Mrs P stopped, aware that she had lost the collective gaze of her female guests, who were all now staring at me.

'Oh!' she yelped, turning. 'I forgot you were coming tonight! How are you, love? I didn't hear the door.'

'Your husband let me in…'

'Where's he gone?'

'I think they sang something about going to the pub.'

'Men! They're always at the pub. Unlike the Rabbit, eh, girls? And at only forty pounds a throw a lot cheaper to keep!'

'YESSSSSSS!' came the collective response.

'Anyway,' Mrs P said, looking at me again, 'how are you?'

'I'm very well,' I muttered, nervously.

'Here,' she said, passing me the Rabbit, 'hold this.'

'Ladies, let me introduce you to my deliveryman ... this is the one I was telling you about. The one who made those lovely Yorkshire puddings.'

'He can mix my puddings any day of the week!' said a huge woman with a moustache and a disturbingly deep voice.

I tried not to catch her eye.

'Anyway I'm glad you're here. I need a hand.'

'I haven't got time.'

'It'll only take a second,' she said, taking the Rabbit from me. 'Could you blow something up for me?'

'Who do you think I am? Guy Fawkes?' I said, with a smile.

It was clear from the silence that my attempt at humour had failed.

'What do you want me to blow up?'

'What do you think?' she said, taking me out into the hall. 'This is an Ann Summers party. I want you to blow up a doll.'

'A doll ... for women?'

'You'd be surprised how lonely we get sometimes,' she said coyly, passing me a large box.

'It's big, isn't it? I've got asthma.'

'Asthma, my arse! Hurry up!'

'What about the delivery?'

'As soon as you've done that, I'll sign and you can go.'

As she closed the door, I began opening the box. It must have taken me ten minutes to blow the bloody thing up and when I had I could barely breathe. Resting against the wall I stared up at it. It was well over six foot. Then I noticed the empty box. Picking it up, I read the label.

THE NEW IMPROVED LIFE-LIKE JOHNNY DEPP. FOR ALL YOUR INTIMATE NEEDS. A LOVER FOR THE BUSY WOMAN OF TODAY! PUMP AND BATTERIES NOT INCLUDED.

Johnny Depp? It looked more like Johnny Morris. Wondering what the world was coming to, I hurriedly began to empty the groceries into the tiny kitchen. Luckily for me, the serving hatch was closed this time. I'd just finished when I realised I still needed a signature. Damn that woman with the wild hair. I knew if I went back in there again she would have me doing something else. I was trapped (again).

Just then, I heard feet descending the stairs. I walked into the hall to find my old friend. Remember the one? The one with the batter?

'Hello,' I said, 'how are you?'

'That's not a local accent,' he said, not at all to my surprise.

'You're right, it's not. Could you please sign here?'

'Certainly.'

Taking the pen from him, I hurried to the door. Before I could reach it, however, he spoke again.

'Oh, hello. Are you a friend of my daughter?'

I turned wearily to give my usual reply – only to find the question was not directed at me.

17

The Blonde and the Coot Pool

I got so friendly with some customers that I even told a few that I was once an actor. Not a good idea.

'Ooh! I'm glad you've come early,' said a lady one night. 'My favourite programme's on in a minute. '

'What's that?' I asked.

'*Grey's Anatomy*. Have you not seen it? It's really good. Some really good acting in it. You used to be an actor, didn't you? I think you'd enjoy it. Actually, there's a British actor in it. What's his name now?' she pondered, scratching her head.

I didn't really care. It was cold, and I could feel the frost penetrating my gloves.

'Hang on. I'll go and check the *Radio Times*.'

'It doesn't matter!' I shouted after her.

Too late. And she still hadn't begun to unload her groceries. It was three minutes before she returned. It doesn't sound much, but when it's minus five, it's an eternity.

'Here it is,' she said, pointing to a photograph of a face I knew well. 'Doctor Owen Hunt, played by ... Kevin McKidd. Says here he's Scottish. You studied in Scotland, didn't you?'

I nodded slowly. What was happening? Why was God doing this to me? WHY ME?

All in all that first full year in the job was not a good one. I came to the conclusion that I'd be driving a van until Judgement Day. Everything was pissing me off: the weather, the roads, my employers, Kevin McKidd's remarkable success and the customers – especially the customers, and, especially, especially, the local students. The lazy students who can't get out of their lazy beds to buy their groceries from a supermarket only metres away from their halls of residence.

*   *   *   *

We deliver to a few colleges and Universities in the area. And at each one there are a few foreign students who, for the most part, are articulate, intelligent individuals, who behave in a most exemplary fashion.

On Tuesday evening, however, I had reason to question this particular college's admissions policy.

It was late and wet and I was tired and wanted to be anywhere but delivering groceries in a van. Then, to make the situation worse, I realised that my final delivery was on a campus. There are many words and phrases that strike fear into a driver's heart. 'Rottweiler' is one; 'stairs' is another; but somewhere near the top of the list is 'halls of residence'.

When I'm put in this situation, I find the best thing to do is give the customer a ring. Find out where they are. Get there as fast as possible and drop the load. Then get out before some drunken, spotty students can strip my van of all its food and drink.

Theory is a wonderful thing.

'Hello, there,' I said in my friendly deliveryman voice. 'I have a delivery for you. Where exactly are you on the campus?'

'Hello?' said the voice at the other end of the phone. It was a female voice, eastern European.

'Yes, hello. I have a delivery for you – can I park near to your room?'

'Hello?'

'Hello,' I said, and then repeated everything I had just said.

'Hello?'

We were getting nowhere. I tried again, but it was just so much wasted breath.

'Hello?'

Oh God.

'Yes, hello – I have a delivery for you.'

'Oh, you have a delivery for me?'

It's at moments like this I wish I had concentrated more at school. What have I done with my life? I repeated the words again.

'Oh, yes,' she said. 'I ordered some groceries for a delivery.'

She said this with a surprised tone. As if booking a home delivery would result in something other than a deliveryman bringing her groceries.

'Oh, I'm glad you came. Why don't you park near my room? It would be easier to unload.'

'That's a very good idea,' I said, with just a tiny hint of sarcasm.

'Okay. There is a small car park near my room. It is near the 'Coot Pool'.'

'Near the what?'

'The 'Coot Pool'.'

'The 'Coot Pool'?'

'Yeeeees! 'The Coot Pool' ... the pool where the coots like to swim.'

Why me?

'Do you mean the lake, love?'

'That is soooo! The lake ... the 'Coot Pool', yes?'

'All right, love. I'll be with you in two minutes.'

Now I had two things to contend with – drunken students and a potential communication breakdown. Thankfully, the 'Coot Pool' wasn't too far away and I was soon pulling up in the car park she had mentioned. Unloading the one tray (that's right, one tray) that probably weighed no more than twenty kilos, I locked the van and pressed the appropriate numbers on the intercom.

'Hello?' said a familiar voice.

'Hello, I've got your delivery.'

'Hello?'

By this point, I was losing the little composure I had left. Just then, thankfully, I heard the buzzer go. Taking my chance, I forced the door open and rushed in. Ahead of me were no less than three fire doors and, at the end, visible through the glass panes, a tall blonde with a big smile and even bigger hair. She was mouthing something. I didn't even have to guess what it was – she only seemed to know one word.

Each of the doors (typically) required me to put down the tray and pull it open. And what did my student friend do? She smiled and waved as I struggled through each one. Muttering under my breath, I pushed on like a contestant from *It's a Knockout*.

'Hello,' she said, when finally I reached her.

'Hello,' I replied, through gritted teeth.

'I must say this is a very fine service you provide,' she said, unloading the tray.

It was then that I noticed the ten tins of hairspray amongst her order and, in its turn, her extraordinary beehive-like hairstyle. It wasn't so much fashioned as sculpted.

'It must be very hard work,' she said, breaking my train of thought. 'Would you like some cack?'

'I'm sorry?'

'Cack. I have some lovely cack. I made it myself.'

At that moment, I wasn't quite sure if I was hearing her correctly – but I found myself battling to keep an awful image out of my mind.

'Your very kind, but I'm a bit busy.'

'It's still warm. It would be nice with a cup of tea, yes? It's got a cherry on the top.'

The penny dropped.

'Oh, cake! Oh, I see – I thought – no, I'm fine.'

'Okay. Will it be you who comes each week?'

Not if I can help it, love.

'Probably not,' I said, with a smile. 'There are quite a few drivers.'

'Are they all as nice as you?' she said, playing with her blonde locks and nearly breaking a finger.

'What are you studying?'

'Law,' she said.

'And will you be going back home when you graduate?'

'Oh, no. I hope to marry a handsome Englishman and practise law in this country.'

Wishing her a good night, I rushed off along the corridor, all the time making a mental note never to murder anyone. Knowing my luck, my defending counsel would be an eastern European with bad pronunciation and very big hair.

18

The Ghosts of Christmas Past

By Christmas time of that second year, I was trying very hard to put away my troubles and enjoy the festivities. I found a little solace in classical music and had the radio tuned into Radio Three or Classic FM most days. One Sunday afternoon, there was a celebration of the music of Malcolm Arnold, who had recently passed away. For those of you unaware of the great man, you may remember he composed the theme to *The Bridge on the River Kwai*, amongst other celebrated film soundtracks. I suppose I took a special interest in the concert because he was born just up the road in Northampton.

On this particular day I had a gap in the middle of the deliveries. We're not allowed to deliver early and sometimes we have to pull over and wait. By chance this day I had pulled onto an airfield that was used heavily during the Second World War. As I stared out across the deserted airstrip and the crumbling control tower on the far side, it began to snow. It was quite a moment, and I was taken completely by the scene before me. Maybe it was because of the music or through the memory of what had happened on the spot all those years ago, but I became angry that nobody seemed to care about these sites. Sites where brave young men and women had changed the course of history.

After a while I did a naughty thing. I fell asleep. And whilst I slept, I dreamt.

* * * *

On the week running up to Christmas, the snow across the south was so heavy it was drifting in places.

Because of the conditions, I was well behind when I made my way to the last address in a small village. It's a place I know well because of the local history. On the outskirts of the village is a disused Second World War airfield, and to those who take an interest in such things (and I'm sorry to say that isn't many) it is a humbling, haunting site.

I don't know exactly how many aircrew lost their lives during the war flying to and from that airfield, but I know it was a fair amount

Often I wonder how many people who pass the airfield each day are aware of the sacrifice.

Even though the snow was still heavy, the moon had somehow appeared through the broken cloud and in its eerie glow I could make out the old control tower by one of the runways. It was an intimidating atmosphere.

As I reached the roundabout near the village, I suddenly heard a deep, resonating sound above me. It was so loud I actually brought the van to a stop on the roundabout. Luckily, there was no traffic. At first I thought it was a helicopter, but then decided that no one in their right mind would be out flying in this sort of weather. Then the sound was gone.

When I reached my final drop I was surprised to find a NOAH (No One At Home). It was odd. Delivery slots at this time of year are like gold dust. I did the usual things. I rang the bell, I phoned; all to no avail. Leaving a card, I drove off.

I was just approaching the roundabout once more when I suddenly heard the sound again, but this time much louder. It sounded very like the engine of an old plane. It was so loud I was sure it was going to crash and slammed on the van brakes. As I did so, I watched in amazement as a figure walked out right in front of me.

Even though I was in a state of shock, the enormity of what had just happened was not lost on me. If it hadn't been for the noise I would almost certainly have run down whoever it was who had just crossed my path.

As the shape made for the old airfield, I turned off the road and jumped out of the van. God knows why – it just seemed the right thing to do. I ran onto the runway and then, to my consternation, saw the figure collapse in the snow. When I caught up, I was startled to find it was an old woman, shaking with cold and mumbling.

'Are they back safe?' she seemed to be saying.

'What?' I said, propping her up in my arms, 'is who safe?'

'The crews. Are they all back?'

I was too stunned to say a thing. Then I was aware of noise in the distance and looked up to see a line of people crossing the roundabout towards the airfield.

'Are they safe?' she repeated.

Don't ask me why, but as the newcomers hurried across the runway towards us, I nodded to her.

'Yes,' she said, pointing towards the dilapidated control tower, 'look – I can see them. They're all back.'

Despite myself, I glanced over and peered through the snow. All I could see was a darkened building. Then I heard another voice.

'Mum, what are you doing?' The woman was middle-aged and distraught. 'You could have been killed.'

As she said this, the other strangers arrived and together we carried the old woman to my van to keep her warm. Shortly after this, she was taken to hospital, leaving me alone with her son-in-law. He explained that running up to the final Christmas before the end of the war the lady's fiancé and his crew had been killed returning from a bombing mission.

Ever since then she had returned to the airfield each Christmas to remember him and to pay her respects. A few months ago, however, she had suffered a stroke and a decision had been made to keep her away this time, to avoid any further stress. But the old girl was wily and had sneaked out, unaware of the treacherous conditions.

I told the man about the noise of the engines. For a while we were both too stunned to say a thing. Instead, we walked over to the old control tower in silence. When we eventually returned to the van something struck me.

'Your name isn't Jones, is it?'

'Yes, it is.'

'I've got a delivery for you.'

Now I knew why there was no one at home.

19

A Deliveryman's Christmas Carol

Maybe it was the time of year, but I was gradually noticing a change in my attitude. I hadn't been aware of it but over those many months, thanks to the people I had met, my attitude to life had changed for the better. From watching and studying people up close, I realised for the first time how similar we all are. Then, to compound this belief, a funny thing happened.

I was delivering to a real tough looking bloke one night. You know the type, broken nose, muscles on his muscles, tough as old boots, that sort of bloke. As he unloaded his groceries he asked me what hours I worked. Telling him I only worked part time, I went on to say that I was a househusband. I expected him to laugh, but to my astonishment, he became quite emotional.

'I wish I had done that?'

'Really?' I said with a smile. I genuinely believed he was taking the piss.

'No, really,' he muttered, his gaze fixed somewhere in the distance. 'I worked away when my kids were growing up. I never really saw 'em. Now I never see 'em at all. They live all over the place. We're not that close. I envy you. I really do.'

On that he wiped a tear from his eye, shook my hand and closed the door. It was quite a moment. It really had an effect on me. I felt a bit like Scrooge. It was as if life had briefly allowed me to see how things may have been under different circumstances.

I was almost born again.

* * * *

The week before Christmas is a living hell for the deliveryman. Not only have we got to contend with the weather, which this weekend has been very wintry indeed, but we also have to put up with the drunken hordes. Have you any idea what it's like when late night revellers want to hug you? Especially big ugly ones called Bill or Frank.

From this, you might begin to understand how we poor drivers don't always slip into the Christmas spirit as quickly as we might. Especially when we have to deliver on Saturday and Sunday evenings. And the weekend just gone was certainly one to remember.

I had a new delivery in Bicester, but for some reason I couldn't find it on the map. I decided to ring them up.

'Hello, is that Mrs Scroggins of 33 School Way?'

'Hey?' said a female voice.

I repeated the question and explained the reason for my call. The problem was, there was so much noise in the background, she could barely hear me.

'Can you lot shut up?' the woman yelled. 'I'm on the phone. What did you say again?"

'I said, I have a delivery for you but I'm having a few problems finding you. You don't seem to be on the map.'

'No, we won't be. It's a 'new build' estate. Where are you now?'

'Broughton Avenue.'

'Oh, you're just round the corner. Go to the end, where you'll see the new houses, then turn right. We're at the very end … you can't miss us.'

On that, she put down the phone and off I went. As I turned at the end of the avenue, I was suddenly blinded by intense light. Whoever I had spoken to was correct in every way. The woman's house was so illuminated by Christmas lights I couldn't miss it. Nobody could. I suspect that at this time of year incoming flights to Luton use it as a marker on foggy nights.

As I pulled up outside the house I marvelled at the glow. It was as if the sun had somehow gone out of kilter and landed in Bicester. Shielding my eyes, I picked my way through the gaudy collection of glowing Santas, reindeer and elves. Even the trees were flashing with red and white fairy lights. Wondering what her electric bill must have been like, I knocked on the door.

After a moment, the door opened to reveal a small boy.

'What do you want?' he growled.

'Is your mum or dad in?' I asked, fighting off the temptation to give him a clip round the ear.

'Me dad's drunk behind the sofa and me mum's snoggin' Uncle Charlie.'

'Well,' I said above the noise of the music that was blaring from the front room, 'when she's finished, could you tell her that her groceries are here?'

Rolling my eyes, I turned to go back to the van, only to find a large elf blocking my way. When I say elf, of course, I mean middle-aged fat bloke dressed as an elf.

'Do want a hand, mate?' he said. It was clear from the way he swayed from side to side he had been drinking.

'No, I'm fine. Aren't you a little lost?'

'How do you mean?' he slurred.

'I mean, shouldn't you be helping Santa? This is his busy week, after all.'

'Oh, no. I phoned in sick,' he said with a laugh.

Presuming he was going to the party, I got to the van and began to unload. When I returned to the house, I found Mrs Scroggins fighting off what I presumed was Uncle Charlie (unless she was popular with ALL her male in-laws).

'Oh, hello,' she said. 'Could you just take it all through to the kitchen? It's the food for the buffet later.'

As I went through, I found myself ambushed by lots of drunken people with streamers – so many, in fact, that by the time I reached the far side of the room my shoulders were so festooned with multi-coloured paper, I could barely move my head. On my return I encountered the elf again, this time carrying a tray of food from the van. I should have told him off, but all I wanted was to get out of there.

When, finally, I'd finished, I searched for Mrs Scroggins and her signature.

'Oh, you can't go yet, love. You've not had a mince pie.'

'I'm in a bit of a hurry.'

'Oh, go on – have a pie and a sherry. It's Christmas!'

'I can't drink and drive...'

'Sherry's not alcohol! I give it to the kids when they get troublesome. Speaking of which, my son Blaine is going to play his recorder in a minute. You have to stay for that.'

Reluctantly, I allowed myself to be steered into the living room and began to consume some seasonal fare.

'Okay everybody, it's the moment we've all waited for. *X-Factor* time!'

Everyone jumped up and cheered. Through the mayhem, I could see the elf waving at me from the other side of the room.

'First up is Blaine. Big round of applause for Blaine!'

All became silent as Blaine began his recital. And what a recital! Although he was playing for about three minutes he only seemed to play two notes. It was a painful experience, but somehow I got through it. Blaine proved himself to be a very plain Blaine, musically at least.

As the applause began I took it as a cue to escape. Big mistake.

'Okay – we have a volunteer!' exclaimed Mrs Scroggins.

'Eh?'

'What are you going to give us, love?'

'I gotta go.'

'I don't know that one. How does it go?' she said, as everyone laughed – and I didn't. 'Come on, we're not letting you go unless you give us a song.'

Oh dear.

Unfortunately, I only know one song all the way through. I've appeared in several musicals. One of my favourites was the musical satire *Oh! What a Lovely War*. One of the songs in that particular show has always stayed close to my heart. 'We'll Never Tell Them' was a popular piece sung by British troops in the trenches. It's a protest song, a very beautiful one, but a protest song nevertheless – not what you might call suitable for a seasonal gathering. But they'd pushed me into it ... so I sang it anyway.

After I'd finished there was complete silence. You could have heard a pin drop. For a moment, I was expecting to hear Simon Cowell's voice telling me I was out of tune or that songs with meaning have no place in modern society.

Instead, I heard sobbing.

'That's the most beautiful thing I've ever heard in my life,' said the elf, clearly overcome with emotion and clearly drunker than he was ten minutes before. From somewhere he had found a bottle of gin.

Wishing everyone a happy Christmas, I ran out to the van. Before I could get in, I realised I'd been followed out by Mrs Scroggins and the elf.

'As if depressing all my guests with your gloomy songs wasn't enough, you've got the audacity to bring a drunken colleague into my house! And he doesn't even look like a real elf!'

She was holding the elf by his collar.

'Colleague? I've never seen him before in my life.'

'Do you mean he's not with you?'

'I thought he was one of your guests.'

'How dare you come into my house, you drunken pig,' she said, hitting the elf over the head with her spare hand.

Almost blind from the glare of the front garden, and concerned that Mrs Scroggins might at any second vent her spleen on me, I jumped into the van and started up the engine. No sooner had I done this, however, than the elf was back.

'Blimey, she's a feisty one!' he said, opening my door. 'Any chance of a lift, guv'?'

'Look - who are you?'

'I was out with my mates but somehow I've lost 'em. We're doing a Christmas pub-crawl. Any chance of a lift?'

'Sorry.'

'Please?'

'I'm not allowed to give lifts.'

'But it's Christmas!'

'Yes, and not a good time to be sacked. Try getting a taxi. That's what they specialise in.'

Wishing the elf a merry Christmas, I drove off to the next address, but couldn't get rid of an unsettling feeling that I hadn't seen the last of him.

After a night of hard slog, including a particularly tough delivery to a top-floor flat, I returned to the store. By then, it was late and snowing heavily and the back gate to the store was closed. It was so cold, I was reluctant to get out and ring the bell, but I had no choice. As I got out, I became aware of banging from the back of the van – the freezer compartment, to be precise. I approached the door cautiously and slowly pulled it open. What I found was a chilling sight indeed.

There, almost white with frost, was a half-frozen elf.

'Bloody hell!' he said, jumping down. 'It's freezin' in there!'

'Well it would be! IT'S A FREEZER, YOU HALFWIT! What were you doing in there? You could have frozen to death!'

'Never mind all that – where are we?'

'Buckingham.'

'Home at last!' he said, giving me a big hug. 'Thank you, Mr Deliveryman.'

'How long have you been in there?'

'God knows. The cold has wiped my memory. Anyway, I gotta go. Merry Christmas. And in the words of Tiny Tim – God bless us, everyone!'

20

The Youth of Today

It was over that Christmas that we discovered that the son of friends of ours had leukaemia. It was terrible news, and it put my whining in perspective once and for all.

I also realised that we're all in the same boat, and that we all have our own problems, and that very few of us actually make it to the top. We all have our dreams and hopes, but do we often achieve what we set out to? I think not. Sure, I acted, and of course it was interrupted by illness – but if I really wanted to, I could go back.

All I know was that on Christmas morning, as I looked at the kids opening their presents and at my wife smiling down at them, I appreciated how bloody lucky I was. God knows why I hadn't seen it before. Now I was just happy to be alive and well, watching my kids grow with my wife at my side.

I had also discovered a love of literature. I don't think I read a book all the way through until I was in my twenties, but, in my forties, I had found an enthusiasm for telling stories and, with hard work, was convinced I could get something published.

During the early part of the new year the amount of snow that fell was incredible. It rarely snows that often around here, but after the heaps of the stuff we found ourselves getting, we began to suspect that the good Lord had been saving it all up specially.

Snow is obviously a problem for we drivers – not only because of the hazards it presents on the roads or because it makes things slippery underfoot. Combined with teenagers, it can be bloody terrifying.

* * * *

Well, what a start we've had to the New Year! The snow has brought Britain to its knees and I haven't made a delivery since Tuesday.

When I left for work that night there wasn't a cloud in the sky, but by the time I'd made my second delivery the counties of Buckinghamshire and Oxfordshire had disappeared beneath a blanket of snow. It was so bad by nine o'clock I couldn't see the road. Any road.

As you should know by now, I don't go in for all this health and safety nonsense. If a job can be done, regardless of the conditions, I'm the man to do it. Luckily for me, my last seven deliveries were in Bicester, which isn't that big. So I went for it.

I'd seen the weather forecast and I knew what was coming, so I'd taken a spare set of clothes. Not that I needed them. Things went well ... well, up until about ten o'clock. I was behind but, thanks to a couple of customers pushing me out of snowdrifts, I was getting the job done. Then I arrived at my final customer. She's a regular and I'm sure she wouldn't mind me observing that she's getting on a bit. So, of course, I was determined to make the delivery.

As I parked the van in an area where I presumed the curb was, I noticed an unsavoury group of teenagers watching me from a small green (or should I say white) in front of her house. I knew what was in their minds. Believe it or not, I was once a teenager.

I got out of the van and was relieved to see them walk off along the road. By this time, the snow had eased and I felt so confident that I could get back to the store in one piece, I suggested I would clear the lady's front path. And that isn't a euphemism, just in case you were wondering.

But, as I cleared the snow, I didn't realise what a fatal error I had made. One of the golden rules for all we deliverymen (and women) is that you always lock your van when you're not in it. This mistake would cost me dear.

It took me about ten minutes to clear the path and, at the end, the lady was good enough to make me a cup of tea. As we chatted, she suddenly made a startling observation.

'Why didn't your friend help you?'

'What friend?' I asked.

'Your friend in the van.'

I looked out of the window. There was someone sitting in the passenger seat. Passing the old lady the tea, I sprinted across the green to the van. I have to admit, the air that night wasn't only white – it was blue as well. When I opened the door I was confronted with a large snowman sitting in my van. Not only that, he was wearing my spare coat, hat and scarf – and a seat belt. Bloody teenagers!

That was only the start of it. When I tried to push the thing out, the damned thing fell apart all over my cab. Despite the situation, I had to smile.

'You all right, mate?' asked an elderly man, who had appeared at the opened door.

'Yes, thanks.'

'I saw the little buggers from across the road. Gawd! I don't know, the youth of today!'

'It's only a bit of snow,' I told him.

'That's not the point! You could have been injured.'

Now, unless I had sat in the snowman's lap for an hour and caught frostbite where the sun don't shine, I couldn't see how I could have been injured at all. But he seemed a decent old bloke so I didn't say anything.

'I mean, ask yourself,' he went on, 'would you have done something like this when you were a teenager?'

'You're right, of course,' I agreed. 'I wouldn't.'

But only because supermarkets didn't do home delivery when I was that age.

21

What's in a Name?

As I glanced at the list of customers one evening, I was amazed to see one I recognised from the literary world. I had seen the lady's name in a list of British literary agents. Here's my chance, I thought to myself. This is it. I will win her over with my louche mancunian charm and then move in with the killer blow – a potted synopsis of one of my novels.

For the rest of the evening I was in a heightened state of excitement. Like an eager teenager on his first date preparing for a night of adolescent joy, I hurried from one customer to the other, blissfully oblivious to the dreadful winter weather. But, when the moment finally came, I didn't get a sweet young thing in a new frock – nor did I find the literary agent of long standing. No. I got a fat bird in a stained nightie telling her husband to 'turn the effing telly down'.

A month before it would have got me down. But not now. Now I was a happy chappy.

* * * *

Prepare yourselves for a shock. Elvis Presley is alive and well and living in Bicester. I should know, I delivered to him on Friday night.

I know what you're thinking. He's finally lost it. After months of staring down at trays of groceries, he's finally lost the plot. Well, bear with me and I will explain.

Each week, my colleagues and I deliver to hundreds, nay, thousands of people across the counties of Buckinghamshire and Oxfordshire. So it's hardly surprising that occasionally we come across odd names – or, in this case, familiar names.

For instance, would you believe me if I told you we delivered to Des O'Connor and Elizabeth Taylor? Or Robbie Burns and Nanette Newman? What about Dick Turpin and Genghis Khan? Well, all right, I made the last two up – but the rest are real people. Honest.

My story begins with one of these familiar names. Now, when I look at the delivery sheet and see the name Des O'Connor, I'm hoping for an elderly man with a false tan who will fall to the ground convulsed with laughter at the most minor witty observation from me. But, believe me when I say this, there is nobody more disappointed than me when a pleasant, pale-faced young man opens the door, happy to see that I've brought him his groceries.

When I looked at my delivery sheet on Friday night, the name that caught my eye was – Tom Jones. That's right, Tom Jones.

Nothing wrong with that, I hear you say. I bet Tom Jones doesn't do his own shopping. If anyone has earned the right to have his groceries delivered, it's our Tom. I mean, it's not as if he's short of a bob or two.

Well, I'm sure he can, and I'm sure he does - but not on Friday night, he didn't, because when I knocked on the door, it wasn't Tom who answered it. No. It was a gentleman looking, sounding and acting not like the 'I-refuse-to-retire-I'll-be-still-singing-when-I'm-a-hundred' Welsh foghorn, but the King himself. One Elvis Presley.

For a moment, I was in a state of shock. Could it really be?

'Mr Jones?' I muttered, my jaw dragging on the ground. 'Mr Tom Jones?'

'That's right,' he said, in a strong Welsh accent – but he wasn't fooling me.

He was a big man and rather fat, with a lip that rose on one side when he spoke. Not only that, as I glanced over his shoulder I could see a white glittery suit hanging on the back of the kitchen door. What really gave it away were the sunglasses. I mean, who wears sunglasses at ten o'clock at night?

Who was he trying to kid? It's the King, I thought to myself. He's tricked us all. He didn't die. He's living on the Bure Park estate in Bicester.

When the initial shock wore off, I looked down at his groceries, and do you know what I saw? Peanut butter, bananas, bacon and honey. Not only was Elvis still alive, but he was still eating the 'Elvis Sandwich'!

You may remember the press blamed the 'Elvis Sandwich' on his downfall. Not that it stopped the rest of America eating them. If you go to the States today you can still see them being consumed (normally by people who die shortly afterwards).

But this was no ordinary man I was dealing with, don't forget – this was the King. It was clear that at some point he had stumbled upon a life-enhancing combination of these normally dangerous ingredients. If this was anyone else they would die in no time eating this sort of thing – but this was Elvis. He'd just laugh in the face of high cholesterol.

'Where do you want your groceries, Elv – I mean, Mr Jones?'

'How much is there?'

'Only this tray.'

'Just empty it here. I'll take it through when you've gone.'

'Are the family out?' I said. It was, of course, a ploy to find out more. I read the papers. Elvis was no fool. He must have known what was coming. He must have known he couldn't remain married to a woman who would one day become a Goth, in her sixties – and as for his daughter: Nicolas Cage? I mean – really! No, believe you me – Elvis got out just in time.

'I live on my own,' he replied, with a sigh.

'Well, it was your choice, Elvis. You can't have any complaints now, cock,' I thought to myself.

But credit where credit's due. The man was a genius. Not only had he bluffed the world – he'd double-bluffed it. Moving to England was good, but moving here and changing his name and accent to that of a British icon was nothing short of brilliant.

It was then that I noticed he was in a neck brace.

'What have you been up to then?' I asked.

'Some idiot ran into the back of me at a pedestrian crossing,' he slurred.

'Are you all right now?'

'I am now ... but at the time I was *all shook up*.'

What did he say? What did he say! Seconds before, he had had my sympathies, but now my view had changed. He was just playing with me.

As I put down the tray, I heard a dog barking from the front room.

'He sounds a big one,' I said.

'Yes, he's a hound.'

'Really? What sort?'

'What do you mean?'

'I mean – what breed?'

For a moment he seemed confused, then he shook his head. *'He ain't nothing but a hound dog*.'

Oh, pleeeeeeeease!

Now I was getting angry, so I decided to call his double-bluff. I started with the white glittery suit.

'That's my nephew's,' he told me. 'I work at a dry cleaners. I get a discount, you see.'

'Okay,' I said. 'Can I ask you why you're wearing sunglasses at this late hour?'

'Why do you ask?'

'No reason.'

He seemed to get quite flustered at this. He knew I was onto him.

'If you must know, I got a couple of black eyes when the car ran into the back of me. Not that it's any concern of yours. I mean, who are you to question me? It's *suspicious minds* like yours that start ugly rumours. If there was *a little less conversation* and a bit more delivering then maybe you could deliver to more people!'

With that, he slammed the door shut. I didn't even get a chance to grab my tray back. Maybe he thought I was about to catch his shoes – well, you know how easy it is to scuff suede.

Okay then, Elvis. I get ya. Your secret's safe with me, pal. But if I don't get a tip at Christmas ... the secret's out!

22

Sexy Sadie

I know what you're all thinking. Where is it? Where's the story about the lonely housewife? The one in the negligée with the big boobs and too much make-up? The one who doesn't care what the neighbours think? Well, I've got a revelation for you ... she doesn't exist. I should know. I've been looking for her for the past year. Just in case my wife happens to be reading this – that was my little joke.

Of course, there are lonely women – ladies who look at me in a certain way from time to time. But, knowing human nature as I do, I realise they aren't the ones that are 'gagging for it', as the 'lad' mags like to put it.

The sensual ones, the passionate ones, the ones with kinky aspirations aren't the ladies with the low-cut tops who bend over ever so slowly to pick up their groceries. No. It's the quiet ones. The ones with the nice houses and pleasant smiles. The ladies with parrots. The ones who talk about politics and literature and 'I hear we're in for a bit of weather.' They're the ones who harbour wicked thoughts about deliverymen, and have a cellar dedicated to the world of bondage.

Or maybe it's all in my head.

* * * *

I've got this customer. She scares me very much. Her delivery is normally on a Sunday afternoon around two. There, in her flat, she waits for me. She's a very naughty girl.

Her name is Sadie. She's a bit of a legend at the store. All the drivers have their stories about Sadie –

about her passion and her vast array of negligées. This is my story.

For the first few months in the job, all I knew of Sadie was her reputation. Then, inevitably, my turn came. Parking up, I glanced across at the flats in question. It was then that I saw a face at the bedroom window. A mixture of excitement and fear grew within me.

I unloaded her single tray of groceries and glanced at the contents. I think it was probably the word 'sexy' that did it for, as I stared down, innuendo took over completely. Cucumber, whipped cream, baby oil, chocolate ... dildos (only joking, we don't sell dildos – yet). I got so excited I could have let go of the tray and still carried it to the door.

Knock, knock, knock.

The curtains at the front window shuddered. I did the same. Then I saw movement in the hall and heard the latch. The door opened and I saw her.

I nearly dropped the tray.

What stood before me was, in the words of Spike Milligan, 'a masterpiece of the embalmer's art'. On top of that she had the most bizarre face I had ever seen. All the features were there, but concentrated in only ten percent of her face. It was difficult to tell, but I was certain she was puckering her lips at me.

Now the wrong side of eighty, she was a tiny, walking bundle of wrinkles and facial hair ... but in a negligée and smoking a cigarette? Luckily, I hadn't eaten.

'Helloooo!' she said. 'I haven't had you before.'

No, and never likely to either, love.

'Where would you like your groceries?'

'Just put them on the doorstep, my darling.'

Her voice was hoarse, from too much smoking. Her skin was incredibly wrinkled and dried out, from too much smoking. She was struggling to breathe, from too much smoking. Her hair was amazingly white, from too much ... age.

With great deliberation, she stuck out her chest suggestively and bent forward. I looked away – but not quickly enough. Well, I say chest: it was more like a hammock, a very saggy, ageing hammock, with a couple of small rocks in it.

'Oh you naughty boy! Are you taking a peek at Sadie's assets?'

Her assets were neither 'fixed' nor 'tangible'. (That's an accountants' joke.)

I counted to ten before I looked down again. Fifteen would have been better. She was bending over again, but now facing the other way.

I began to feel faint.

'Here's your tray, dearie,' she muttered breathlessly (I hoped it was the cigarettes).

'Here, I'm all alone at the moment,' she said, glancing up and down the street, 'do you fancy a bit?'

I had no idea which bit she was offering, but I was pretty certain I didn't want any of it.

'No, thanks.'

'What's the matter? Don't you find mature ladies attractive?'

Mature, yes. Ancient, no.

Just then I was aware of a presence at my side. I turned to see a large man covered in tattoos.

'Sadie go in side!' He growled.

I couldn't help but notice he was giving me a very nasty stare. As Sadie disappeared into the flat, the man walked into the hall and turned to face me. I had a rather nasty feeling he was about to thump me. But instead, to my surprise, he smiled.

'Don't blame yourself, son. I know what effect she has on men. She's a cracker isn't she? A real beauty! I have to fight 'em off some days. But it's worth it to have her in my life.'

'You're very lucky,' I said, only revealing a tiny bit of sarcasm.

'She used to be a dancer, you know? You may not have noticed, but she's got beautiful legs.'

'Takes the focus from her face,' I thought to myself.

'She was nearly in Pan's People, you know?'

'Really?' I said, quite shocked.

'Oh, yes. Do you know what stopped her?'

'Her ugliness,' I wondered.

'Too short.'

23

Three Colours Pink

As I drive my van, my mind wanders. Like balloons in the breeze, thoughts flutter in the vast empty space that is my brain. Sometimes these thoughts mingle and from their shape I see things. Not stories, as such. Observations would be a better description. People. Places. Experiences.

Driving through the country lanes I sometimes see people running, or farmers at work, or children on their bikes. Sometimes they wave and I wave back. It's as if we have made some type of contact through the windscreen. Nothing's said. It's as if we're all connected in some way.

*   *   *   *

There are many women in my life, but – just in case she may be reading this – only one that I truly love.

Of course, there is a great deal of love for my mother and sisters, not to mention my sisters-in-law and aunts and cousins and nieces. I even have enough to spare for my female friends, but there are others who I barely know who enrich my life each day.

Take Mrs R of Bicester. She is old and frail. She's survived the Second World War, the loss of her husband and recession – and I mean proper recession, not the half-arsed one we've got now. In her day, people struggled to feed their families, not their mobile phones. I deliver to her most weeks. She always has a smile for me. She never moans. She never complains. She says (and I believe her when she says it) 'that she can't grumble'. She wouldn't know how.

She is an example to idle teenage mums everywhere. Maybe I'm generalising ... but then maybe I'm not. I deliver to them as well.

She doesn't know it, but Mrs R is important to me. Sometimes she is the reason I smile when I don't want to.

There are others too. After dropping the kids off at school, I sometimes take the long way home. If I'm lucky, I may see the district nurse struggling up the hill on her bike. Her arse and thighs are so big the saddle is almost invisible. Nevertheless, there is something wonderfully erotic about a large lady in uniform gasping for breath. Like Mrs R, she brings a smile to my face.

There's another. I find her on the high street – not literally, you understand. You see, we have this funeral parlour. There's nothing particularly special about it. It has wreaths, it has lilies, it has cleanliness, and it has that sombre tone inherent to such places. But this one has a lady. She sits at a desk in front of an ancient computer screen. I don't know her name and she's too far away for me to judge her age, but there is something about her distant gaze that makes my heart sink each time I pass. Day after day, she stares out into a world that ignores her. She sees the people as they go by, but nobody ever looks back. Perhaps they see her as the personification of death, and to catch her eye even for a second would bring an unimaginable end to their lives.

I feel for the lady in the funeral parlour.

But maybe I'm wrong. Maybe it's all an illusion. Maybe she thinks wicked thoughts about the people who ignore her. Maybe she has urges to take off her clothes and run wild through the coffins and lilies. Or maybe she's like me and finds the people who pass by important features in her life. People like the district nurse with the huge arse, or the strange man with the sympathetic smile who passes by from time to time.

24

Superstitious, Moi?

Now life was a joy. I was enjoying my children, my wife, everything. Nothing could get me down. It was as if I really was reborn. Amazing what driving a van can do.

Delivering to a lady in Brackley one day, I was amazed to hear her say that she couldn't sign for her delivery with red ink. At first I thought she was winding me up. I mean what an odd thing to say. Then she explained why, and I found the explanation good enough for a story.

* * * *

Delivered to a lovely lady yesterday. We had a nice chat. I mentioned my writing and she seemed interested. Goes without saying that I asked if she was a publisher or not. She wasn't.

When it was time to move on I passed her my pen and asked her to sign on the dotted line, but to my astonishment she threw up her arms and refused, point blank.

'Why?' I asked.

'Because it's red,' she said.

'Is that important?' I replied.

'It is if you're Chinese.'

'But you're not,' I observed. 'Chinese, I mean.'

'That's not the point!' she said, as she went to find another pen.

It was all very strange, but she was pretty, so I didn't say anything.

When she returned, I cross-examined her on the red ink situation. The answer? The Chinese believe that

signing your name with red ink is velly – sorry, very – bad luck.

'Why is it bad luck?' I asked.

'It just is.'

I couldn't argue with that.

Now, I'm not that superstitious but the way my luck has been over the years, I'm willing to listen to anything. What puzzles me about superstition is the mechanics of it all. I mean, who comes up with it all? Who was the individual who decided signing your name with red ink is bad luck? Was it some bloke who got a bit bored one day? An old soothsayer who was being sidelined by some new kid on the block? Did he just make it up to impress the locals? Is the one about 'never walking under ladders' a riposte from the other fella? It's all very confusing.

'Have you always been this superstitious?' I said.

'I wasn't until I got married. My ex-husband was very much that way inclined.'

'I see.'

'Oh, yes,' she muttered, staring off into the distance. 'Saved our lives once.'

'Really?'

'We were going to Milton Keynes to do a bit of last-minute Christmas shopping, when this black cat ran across the road in front of us.'

'What happened?'

'Well, my husband knew better than to cross its path, so he did a handbrake turn.'

'In the middle of the road? Blimey! So he believed that not crossing the path of the black cat and going the other way would keep away the bad luck?'

She nodded.

'So you avoided bad luck that day?'

'We did ... but the cat didn't. We were going that fast that when we turned round we ran over it going the other way.'

How I didn't laugh I don't know.

'So how did it save your life?' I asked, rather confused.

'Later that day, the café we normally eat in served spinach soup.'

'Yeeeees?' I responded, now thoroughly bewildered.

'I'm allergic to spinach,' she explained. 'I once had some by mistake and went into a coma for three days.'

'But, surely, if you're allergic to spinach you wouldn't have had the soup.'

'Yes, but – as my husband pointed out at the time – we were so troubled after the cat incident, we may not have noticed.'

It seemed pointless arguing with her.

'I could read your fortune, if you like,' she said.

'Really?'

'Oh, yes. I'm very gifted in that area.'

'Do you read tea leaves?' I enquired.

'I do, actually. Come in. You know a bit about it yourself then, do you?'

No, love ... but I know you've got to make a cup of tea before you can do it.

25

The Deliveryman

I still couldn't get an agent or a publisher, but now I didn't care. For the first time, I was grateful that I had the time to write. Now I had everything in perspective.

One night I delivered to a pregnant lady. I suggested bringing the groceries through, but she was having none of it. Of course, being a bloke I was very worried that lifting something heavy might bring on a premature birth. It didn't. But the moment did give birth to a story.

* * * *

Last night was a night I will never forget.

It was dark when I reached the small cottage. I was half an hour late and wanting nothing more than my bed. The reason I was late was because my sat nav could not find the address of a new delivery.

On most new deliveries, especially ones in the middle of nowhere, the customer tends to give some instructions on how to find them, especially if the delivery is after dark. But not this one.

Parking up the van, I unloaded and made my way to the house. After a short wait, a very heavily pregnant lady appeared at the door.

'Good evening,' I said.

'Hello. Any trouble finding me?'

'No problems at all,' I told her. 'Okay, everything's there – now, where would you like me to put it?'

'Put it down there and I'll carry it through.'

'Are you sure,' I replied, pointing to her huge belly.

'Oh, never mind that. That's not due for another two weeks.'

'But ...'

'But nothing. I'm a farmer's daughter. I'm pregnant, not paralysed.'

'Well, if you're sure.'

So off I went to the van for the rest of her stuff. When I returned, I found the farmer's daughter somewhat changed.

'Are you all right? You look a bit pale.'

'My – waters have broken,' she gasped, in a total state of shock.

'You didn't order any water,' I replied, glancing at her invoice.

'No ... MY WATERS HAVE BROKEN!'

'Oh, my God!' Now I was in a state of shock. 'I'll phone for an ambulance.'

'I don't think there'll be time. Besides, this is a very difficult place to find in the dark.'

Tell me about it.

Now, I have to say I have been in many dodgy situations in my life. I grew up on a council estate in Manchester. I've seen horror up close. I know what it looks like. But I think I can safely say I have never been so terrified in my life as I was in that moment. It was panic time. Panic time with ribbons and coloured balloons and dancing dogs.

'We need towels and hot water!' I said, pushing her down the hall.

'What for?'

'I don't know, but that's what they always use in films.'

'This isn't a film! This is real life! I'm having a baby!'

'Well, I didn't think it was wind, did I!'

Sitting her on the sofa, I tried to calm the situation.

'Look, where's your husband?'

'I'm not married.'

'Well, the father then?'

'Never met him.'

'Unless your name is Mary, you must have met him once!'

'There's no need to shout! It happened whilst I was on my holidays. Me and me friend got a last-minute deal in Lloret De Mar. We had a week there...' she said, her mind elsewhere for a moment or two. 'Could have been one of seven.'

I rolled my eyes, but this was no time for a debate on social decline.

'Oooooooh!' she said, breaking my train of thought. 'I think it's coming!'

'What – now?'

'I think so!'

'It can't come now!'

'It can do what it bloody likes! Quick, get me knickers off!'

'What!'

'Unless you want it to fight its way through a yard of elasticised nylon, I suggest you do what needs to be done!'

Closing my eyes, I did indeed do what needed to be done. When I got a job as a deliveryman I didn't think I would be doing it literally.

Now, I have children myself. I was even present at their births. It was a remarkable experience. But that was with my wife, a woman I've known for quite some time, in a hospital. Not in a remote cottage with a complete stranger. Even though I knew it was going to be too late, I rang for an ambulance. I also called her sister, who lived about twenty miles away. Then, having filled a bowl with hot water, and having gathered some towels, I knelt before my new friend as she lay back on the sofa.

'Okay,' I said. 'What's your name?'

'Sue.'

'Well, Sue. I'm Lee – and this is going to be quite an experience for both of us. Are you ready?'

'I'm scared, Lee,' she said, fighting back tears.

'Well, if it's any consolation, I am too. You have to be strong. Do you hear me? You can do this. I've only known you ten minutes, but it's clear to me that you've got something about you. You're going to be fine. I know it. Now, are you ready?'

'Yes...Ohhhhhhhhh!'

'Okay ... I've been in this situation before. I've got kids myself. All you have to do is push.'

'Push what?'

'I don't know ... just push!'

'I can't push if I don't what I'm pushing!'

'When my wife was having a baby, the midwife said it was a bit like having a big poo.'

'I'M NOT HAVING A POO. I'M HAVING A BABY. AND THIS IS A NEW SOFA!'

'That's the least of your concerns. It must be a bit like that though - you know, similar muscles ... similar sensation.'

Then the situation changed.

'Oh, my god! I can see something!' I said.

'Ohhhhhh!'

'Don't panic ... it's a head! That's good! It means it's the right way round. Now push! PUSH! HAVE A BIG POO. HAVE A POO, SUE. THAT'S IT. IT'S COMING!'

And so it was there in that little cottage, on a wet Wednesday evening, that a new life came into the world. Amongst the screams and blood and God knows what else, a child was born.

'You've done it, Sue! You've done it!' I said, putting the little fella on a towel.

'What is it, Lee?'

'It's a baby!'

'Could you be more specific?'

'It's a boy!'

'Oh! I always wanted a boy!'

'No hang on, that's the umbilical cord ... it's a girl!'

'Oh! I always wanted a girl!'

Talk about hedging your bets.

'There you are...' I said, putting the wailing girl into her arms. 'What are you going to call her, mum?'

'I don't know,' she said, as tears rolled down her cheeks. 'I was too scared to think of a name in case something went wrong.'

'That's understandable.'

'But I think I'll call her Anne, after my mum ...' Then she stopped and looked down at me. 'No, I won't ...I'll call her Leanne, then I'll always remember you.'

26

Coalition

I meet a lot of people who treat me with the respect I deserve. But there are a lot who look down their noses at me. I'll give you an example. I delivered to a large house in the country one night. The couple were polite (in a very condescending way) but clearly wanted me out of the way a.s.a.p. Having forced me to walk all the way around the back of the house so as not to damage the shagpile, I was then obliged to stand in silence as they unloaded the groceries onto the kitchen table. It was an interesting five minutes. I've never been invisible before.

'Well, if he's not in *Henry V*, his name is certainly mentioned.'

'I think you're right ... and what about *The Merry Wives of Windsor*?'

'Yes, but I'm sure he's in another one as well.'

I knew who they were talking about and wanted to tell them the answer. I just decided that rudeness didn't deserve a reward.

'Oh, for god's sake!' exclaimed the lady as she glanced over her receipt. 'Why have you substituted quails' eggs for ducks'? Have you no sense of scale? We're having a dinner party on Saturday evening and how can I give my guests ducks' eggs as an hors d'oeuvre? It's scandalous!'

'I'm sorry,' I said, trying to calm the situation. 'Sometimes that happens. The pickers are usually quite pushed for time.'

'That's no excuse.'

'I appreciate that, but it does explain why it may have occurred. Or maybe it's because they'd never seen a quail before. We have a lot of foreign students.'

'Bloody foreigners!' said her husband.

I waited for him say something else, but nothing came. Having apologised for the upset the eggs had caused, I put them under my arm and made my way to the door.

'It's a lovely house you've got,' I said, never one to leave a customer on a bad note. 'Is it Edwardian?'

Laughing in unison, they glanced at each other. 'No, dear. Georgian.'

'Well, whatever period, it's very beautiful.'

'You wouldn't say that if you had to pay for the upkeep,' the woman muttered as she opened the door.

'My heart bleeds for you, love,' I thought to myself.

'Oh, by the way,' I said as I got outside. 'He's also in *Henry the Fourth* Parts One and Two.'

'Who?'

'Falstaff. He appears in four plays in all. *Henry the Fourth* Parts One and Two, *Henry V* and *The Merry Wives of Windsor*.'

'How could you possibly know that?' said the husband, joining his wife by the door. 'You're a van driver.'

'You'd be surprised,' I replied. 'I can also spell my name and go to the toilet by myself.'

Luckily I didn't get sacked for my sarcasm. So I used it as a basis for another story.

* * * *

2010 turned out to be a particularly historical year for us British. We had acquired our first coalition government since the war – and that wasn't the only change either. Me and the lads (and the girls) had been given a new delivery area. Although we were keeping north Bucks we were saying goodbye to south Northants, and hello to north Oxfordshire. I was very excited. As you know, in the year since I started I had gone to great lengths to find myself a literary agent or publisher, but if there are any in Northamptonshire, we don't deliver to them. However, I told myself, who knows what delights north Oxfordshire may hold?

It was out with the old and in with the new...

My first delivery in Oxfordshire was in a place called Piddington. The trouble was, I'd never been to that part of the country in my life. It's lovely – very green, very leafy. The sort of place where you imagine fairies and pixies dance beneath the dense canopy. (Well, it is if you're slightly unstable like me.) Unfortunately, the foliage is so dense the satellite that communicates with my sat nav couldn't see through it.

So there I was, completely lost, driving down this narrow country lane. After a minute or so, I saw this Land Rover coming towards me. I flagged it down.

'Excuse me,' I asked the driver. 'I'm looking for Piddington.'

'This is a private road!' said a rather chubby, red-cheeked chap in a tweed jacket.

'Sorry, I didn't realise.'

'Can't you read, man?'

I told him I could, which did nothing to calm his temper.

'Piddington is straight ahead, but I'm buggered if I'll allow "Johnny" supermarket to use it as a short cut. Now, off with you, before I report you to your supervisor. I'm the local MP, I'll have you know, and I carry a lot of weight around these parts!'

He did as well, about eighteen stone.

So off he went, three shades redder than he was before he spoke to me. And me? Well, even though Piddington was only a mile or so ahead, I had to reverse nearly a mile down a very narrow country lane. I was not very happy. In fact, in my angry state, I could almost hear the pixies laughing at me.

But they wouldn't have the last laugh – and neither would my chubby Member of Parliament. Because, within a week, I would have my revenge.

The election came and went and nobody was any the wiser about who was in charge. Mr Brown had a good stab at barricading himself in but, in the end, the outcome was decided by a Liberal Democrat. Now, how many times can you say you've heard that before?

A couple of days later, I was back in Oxfordshire, only a few miles away from the incident with the MP.

Again I was on a quiet country lane, and again I was lost. Governments may come and go, but my sense of direction will never improve.

Realising the lane I was on led nowhere, I decided to turn round. But as I began to do so, I saw a car in the ditch just ahead. I drove forward to see if there was anyone inside and I was astounded to establish three things:

1. It was not a car; it was a Land Rover.
2. It was not in the ditch, but on the other side.
3. There was someone in it.

Yes, you guessed it. My chubby MP friend from the previous week.

Coming to terms with what I was seeing, I stumbled across the ditch to the vehicle, to find my red-faced friend flustered, but okay. I took off his seat belt and helped him out.

'Are you all right?' I asked.

'Damned deer ran out in front of me. Nearly hit the damned thing.'

'You must have travelling at some speed to get the car all the way across the ditch.'

'I was in a hurry, damn you! Now, never mind your impudence, just give me your phone!'

'I beg your pardon?'

'I need your phone. It's important. Me battery's run out and I need to get to London for a very important meeting with the Prime Minister!'

For a moment I just looked at him. A wicked thought entered my mind.

'This is rather a unique situation, isn't it?'

'How do you mean?'

'I mean, what do I get out of it?'

'What?'

'I think you know where I'm coming from. As I see it, this phone call is essential to your success. If you've got an appointment with the Prime Minister, it must be very important. I mean, it would be embarrassing if you couldn't make it. For all I know, he could be offering you a cabinet position. It would be awful to miss the moment, wouldn't it?'

'I don't know what you're playing at, you scoundrel, but this isn't the time for joking. Just give me your damned phone!'

I gave him a smile. 'Okay, I'll give you my phone. I'll even give you a lift to the station. But only on one understanding. That you allow my colleagues and I to access Piddington through your estate.'

'What? You ...'

'Temper, temper,' I said, waving the phone in his face. 'Take a leaf out of your leader's book. Sometimes it makes sense to swallow your pride and take what's on offer. That way you don't end up with nothing. Or would you rather we got our negotiating teams in?'

'All right, you swine. It's a deal!'

I didn't believe him, so I wrote up a quick contract on the back of an old invoice. I titled it 'Manifesto for Change'. He didn't like it, but he signed it. So did I. I didn't use my real name, though. I called myself Lee Clegg. He didn't like that, either.

Later that night, I saw him on *Newsnight*. He looked very pleased with himself, but not as pleased as I was the following week when I waved to him on his patio as I cut through his estate.

27

The Mighty Billy Baize

I meet quite a few *characters* doing my job. Funny people, artistic people, sarcastic people, melodramatic people. As I've said before it's odd how important they become over time, especially when you realise how little time you spend with them. I became fond of one particular customer. He even inspired me to write a story about him.

*   *   *   *

I've got this customer: his name's Billy. Billy Baize. He's a funny guy. No, really – he's a funny, funny guy. I was with him yesterday. As much as I love the man, though, he can be rather draining.

'Well, I never. The deliveryman cometh! Do you get it? Put it there, son,' he said as he offered his hand and a beaming smile washed across his face.

I took the hand nervously. The last time I did so, I got an electric shock. You see, Billy is a comedian. Well, WAS would be a more precise description. He's in his nineties now. Not that you'd think that, to look at him. The way he hops around entertaining his few visitors is a joy to see.

'Here's a good one. What's red and sits in the corner? Eh? Any ideas? A naughty strawberry. Eh? Eh? Do you like it? Cor, I gotta thousand of 'em. Here's another. A bloke goes to the doctor and says "Doc, I've got a lettuce stuck up my arse." The doctor has a feel about and says "I'm sorry, sir, but this is just the tip of the iceberg." Come on, be honest! Eh? Eh?'

I love Billy. It's simply impossible to leave his house without a smile on your face.

A few months ago, I was talking to his daughter. She told me that Billy first went on stage at the age of seven. Over the years, he's shared the bill with the likes of Max Miller, Arthur Askey and the Crazy Gang, who, unlike a lot of today's entertainers, worked endlessly to hone their acts.

But when I'm with Billy I also get a sense of loss, for a world of entertainment that's dwindled away. The truth of it is, we don't go out anymore. We sit in and watch the TV or surf the web. Either way, because of it people like Billy don't exist anymore.

'I've got to go, Billy,' I said, making my way to the door.

'All right, son. I'll give you one for the road, one from the greatest that ever lived. The Cheeky Chappy himself, Max Miller:

"There was a little girl
Who had a little curl
Right in the middle of her forehead;
And when she was good, she was very, very good,
And when she was bad ... she was very, very popular."

'I thang you!'

There's a sad footnote to this story. A few weeks ago, the man who inspired me to write this story passed away. This happens a lot. We deliver to a lot of elderly people. You probably experience it yourself. What about the old lady you used to see at the supermarket on a Wednesday morning but who is no longer there, or the nice old man who used to sit at the bar in your local. The one who always acknowledged you with a smile?

A customer muttered a phrase to me a few days after his death. It's stayed with me ever since.

'You're a long time dead. Enjoy it while you can.'

I know my elderly friend did.

28

An Eligible Man

As I've already said, I deliver to an awful lot of elderly people. Most of them are lovely. The only problem is – which isn't really their fault – is their lack of urgency. If it was up to me I'd let them take all day putting their shopping away, but unfortunately my employers only allow me thirty seconds a tray. Now when you consider that tray has to go from my van to the customer's kitchen to be unloaded and returned again, that isn't a lot of time.

Now consider what it must be like for an elderly person. Their concept of time is different from mine. They have more pressing concerns. They often get confused and worried. The last thing they need is a delivery driver giving them a hard time. So I, and the majority of my colleagues, go out of my way to help. I just wish my employers were a little more understanding.

At one particular address I deliver to regularly, live two elderly sisters. I jokingly call them my girlfriends. We always have a laugh. One day, more to embarrass me than anything else, they asked me to dance. I didn't, but it gave me a great idea for a story.

*   *   *   *

I was in Buckingham yesterday. Some parts of the town are very old and, being a fan of all things ancient, I'm never happier than when delivering to some ageing tenement older than Dickens. Or a cottage that was standing before Shakespeare picked up a quill. Imagine what stories bricks and mortar could tell us.

Anyhow, yesterday I found myself knocking on the door of a rather grand house in the centre of the town.

At first there was no reply and I was about to knock again when I heard giggling behind me.

'Hello, Mr Deliveryman!' said voices in unison.

I turned to see two elderly ladies; they must have been in their eighties. I'm no historian, but what they were wearing must have been just as old if not older. Telling myself it was probably for a fancy dress party, I descended the steps to greet them.

'Good morning, ladies,' I said with my normal deliveryman charm.

'Good morning!' they replied, giggling like teenagers.

'Do you live here?'

'We do Mr Deliveryman!'

'Good,' I said with a roll of the eyes. 'And where would you like your groceries?'

'Would you bring them to the rear?' said one, cuddling the other. 'That way we can unpack and admire your muscular frame!'

'Oh, Maude, don't encourage him!'

'I can't help it,' Maude replied, as they giggled once more and hurried to the back of the house.

Rolling my eyes again, I began to unload.

The house was huge. It had three floors and must have contained at least a couple of dozen rooms. The garden was even more impressive. At the bottom, it actually had an enormous hot house that Kew Gardens would have been proud of.

Entering the large kitchen, I found the gigglers once more.

'Just place them on the table and Maude will unpack,' said the taller of the two. 'I shall tick the list.'

Hoping she was a fast ticker, I returned to the van for the rest of their groceries. As I placed the final two trays on the table, I watched as they worked their way methodically through the items. When they were done, Maude, whom I suspect was the younger of the sisters, whispered in the other's ear. Her sister giggled uncontrollably.

'Maude would like to know if you are a good dancer.'

'Well, I have been known to strut my stuff from time to time,' I said, with a wink.

Suddenly they became very serious.

'I don't mean vulgar dancing, Mr Deliveryman. I was referring to the sophistication of the waltz.'

'Oh, sorry. Well, I did try it once ... but I wasn't very good.'

'Pity ... you are tall with a slim waist, the perfect requirements for a dancer. We'll see what we can do.'

I didn't like the sound of that. However, I didn't have time to think any more of it as Maude was whispering again. The result? More giggling.

'You're right, dear, he does have a look of Mr Forsyth. Are you a fan of the ballroom dancing on the television?'

'Can't really say I've ever watched it.'

By the look on their faces it was clearly not the answer they were hoping for.

'I hope you are not a fan of the *X Factor*, Mr Deliveryman?'

'Oh God, no,' I said, beginning to feel the strain of their combined stares. 'From what I've heard it's full of talentless no-hopers.'

'Quite so,' she said, clearly happy with my reply.

'Well, if that's everything, I think I'd better be getting on.'

'Oh, but you can't go yet …'

'I've got other deliveries …'

'You must stay for tea.'

Vainly I attempted to explain that I'd only just started the run and that I really must be going – but they had other things in mind.

'No, no, no. You can't possibly go until you've refreshed yourself ... and danced with Maude.'

Oh dear.

Quickly clearing away the table and chairs from the centre of the room, the sisters disappeared, only to return a few moments later with a colossal gramophone. Placing it on the table, which was now in front of the door and thus blocking my escape, I was led onto the makeshift dance floor.

'What shall we start with Dorothy?'

'We will begin with a Viennese waltz, dear,' Dorothy replied. 'I realise this can be rather daunting for a beginner, but no matter. I'm sure you will try your best, Mr Deliveryman.'

Why does this always happen to me? Why can't I get flat tyres or get stuck in muddy fields like the rest of the drivers? Why can't I say 'Oi! Mad women! I need to go!' It's probably due in no small part to my pleasant nature.

'Ladies – I have to go. I don't have time for this,' I said, beginning to move the table from the door.

'But it won't take long,' they said in unison, pulling me back.

I resisted but, despite their years, they had the strength of oxen.

'This is not what we expect of a gentleman,' said Maude, wrapping her arms tightly around me.

'I'm not a gentleman!' I protested, trying to break her hold. 'I'm a deliveryman! There is a difference, you know!'

No sooner had I finished the sentence than I heard an orchestra strike up.

'Take your places, please,' said Dorothy – but still I held back. 'Very well, Mr Deliveryman ... one dance and you may go.'

'One dance?' I said through gritted teeth.

'One dance.'

I treated the whole experience like being at the dentist. The sooner it was out of the way the better. Of course, it was a disaster. I spent more time stepping on Maude's toes than I did actually dancing. Oddly, though, my partner didn't seem to mind. With her eyes closed and a broad smile on her face, she was in her element. Clearly, the old girls had been deprived of male company for too long. When the music stopped, Maude curtsied elegantly, forcing me into a stiff, embarrassed, bow.

Relieved it was all over, I made for the door.

'Oh, you dance divinely,' said Maude, pulling me back. 'One more dance, please!'

'NO!' I shouted, pulling my arm free. 'ENOUGH IS ENOUGH. I GOTTA GO!!!'

Suddenly, all was silent. Quite taken aback by my outburst, Maude rushed to Dorothy's side.

'Mr Deliveryman, there is no need for such ungentlemanly behaviour!'

'I'm sorry. I didn't mean to shout – it's just that I have to go.'

'How dare you! Not only have you upset my sister, you have disgraced your profession.'

There was a loud banging from above.

'And now look what you have done. You have woken father.'

FATHER? They had a father still living? Or maybe the place was haunted?

'I have every right to report you to your manager,' warned Dorothy before rushing off.

As her footsteps sounded on the stairs I tried to apologise to Maude for my outburst. Before she could reply, however, Dorothy reappeared at the door.

'Father would like to speak with you.'

'I don't think you're quite appreciating my predicament here. I have other customers to deliver to. I really have to go.'

'Very well then, go ... and I will ring your manager.'

The old bugger had got me. She knew it as well. I could see it in her eyes. There was only one way out now.

'Okay ... lead me to Old Father Time.'

In the bedroom, not unnaturally, I found a bed with someone lying in it. The bed was huge and as old as the house. The occupant was male and possibly even older.

'Where is he? I can't see him. Where is he? Is he here? Help me up!' squeaked the figure.

From the mass of freckles, hairless skin and toothless gape, I suspected the old man was well into his second century. There was an odd smell about him too. Maybe he had already started to decompose, to save time later?

As Maude scurried around the bed to help him up, Dorothy pushed me to the foot of the bed.

'Is he here?' demanded the old man again.

'He's at the bottom on the bed, father,' said Dorothy.

'I can't seem him! Get him to wave!'

'Could you possibly wave?' she enquired.

I waved feebly.

'Is he waving?'

'I think you need to be a little more dynamic than that,' said Dorothy.

Despite myself, I did as suggested.

'There he is – I see him now! Where are the girls?'

'I am by the door, and the supporting hand on your back is Maude's.'

'I thought as much ... feeble it is. Women are feeble. Have I told you that?'

'Many times, father,' replied Dorothy, with a sigh.

'Now then, young feller ... I say, you *are* young, aren't you?'

'I'm nearly forty-five.'

'What's he say?'

'You'll need to speak up,' said Dorothy.

'I'm nearly forty-five!' I shouted.

'Where's he gone now?'

'You'll need to keep waving your arms,' Dorothy told me.

'I said, I'm nearly forty-five!'

I was now shouting very loud and flapping like a parrot.

'Forty-five? Whooo! You're a child!' the old man shrieked with a laugh. 'When I was in me forties, Herr Hitler was trying to invade Buckingham. I stopped him, though. I showed him!'

'Father was in the Home Guard,' said Maude, proudly.

'What she say?'

'Your daughter said you used to be in the Home Guard!' I shouted.

'Are you? I used to be in the Home Guard! It's nice to know they've kept it going. Keeps you young 'uns out of mischief!'

I suppose I should have clarified the misunderstanding, but with all the arm waving I was getting quite tired.

'Now then, I suppose you'll be wondering why I called for you, eh?'

'It had crossed my mind,' I muttered.

'What's he say?'

Dorothy glared over at me.

'I said, yes, I did wonder!'

Suddenly the old man began to cough, violently, forcing me to flap back out of range. Then, as suddenly as it had started, it stopped.

'Well, it's quite simple,' he said, wiping his mouth with the bedclothes, 'as you have probably worked out, I am not long for this world. And before I go I need to make arrangement for these young girls.'

Despite my best efforts, a smile found its way to my lips. It was duly noted by Dorothy. Somehow I forced the smile away.

'Arrangements?' I asked.

'A husband! Every man needs a wife. But in this instance you'll be getting two for the price of one!'

I wondered if I'd misheard him. Did he say 'you'? He did, you know. And did he mention marriage?

'They're fine women. They may look old. You may even be thinking they're beyond child-bearing years ... but it's amazing what medical science can do. What with all this PVC and articulated insemination, you'll be churning 'em out! And they'll make you happy. Oh, yes. Their mother was wonderful in the bedroom department...'

'Sorry – can I just stop you there? Just for a moment?' Bringing my arms to a gradual stop, I took a step closer to the bed. 'What are you talking about?'

'What's he say?'

I took another step. 'I said, what are you talking about? Why are you going on about marriage when I'm already married and – I'VE GOT TO GET ON!'

'You're shouting again!' said Maude, cuddling her father. 'How dare you shout at dear papa!'

'Get off me, woman! Did he say he was married?'

'That's right!' I shouted back.

'You already have a wife?'

'That's right – and two children.'

'Oh, that's nothing. I once had a pal who had six wives. His sex life was never mundane. He had twenty-five kids!'

'That's bigamy.'

'What do you mean, that's big of him? He was a fine fellow, I'll have you know. African, as I remember. It's very popular over there. They have competitions.' Suddenly his tone changed. 'Now look here, I'm not asking for much. Just take these beautiful girls off my hands, give me some piece of mind, eh? I'll even throw in my allotment.'

From time to time, I do lose my temper. But I can safely say I have never been so angry as I was that day.

'I'll tell you what I'll do,' I muttered through gritted teeth. 'If you open the door and let me out, and you don't say another word about marriage and children, I promise I won't ring the police and tell them you have kidnapped me. How about that, eh?'

I should have been uncomfortable with the tone I had adopted. It was a sackable sort of tone, a 'we-don't-talk-to-our-customers-like-that-because-we-don't-want-the-bad-press' sort of tone. Somehow I managed to get a grip and forced myself to the door … only to find Dorothy.

'Where's he gone now!' the old man shouted.

Maude was about to say something, but Dorothy put up her hand and stopped her. Her eyes were fixed on mine now. Then she spoke.

'He's gone, father.'

Slowly, she moved away from the door, allowing me to go downstairs. As I moved the table away from the outside door, I realised she had followed me down.

'I'm sorry,' she said. 'He gets carried away. It's always like this. You see, we don't get many visitors. Please don't call the police.'

'I have no intention of calling the police. I just need to get on. I'm sorry for shouting.'

'That's all right,' she sighed, opening the door. 'It was nice to have met you.'

'It was nice to meet you too, Dorothy ... you should go out occasionally. Find yourself a man.'

'Who would have an old spinster like me?'

'You'd be surprised. If I wasn't a married man … and fifty years older ... and able to dance...'

The smile that spread across Dorothy's face was a joy to see. As I walked back to the van a neighbour popped his head over the fence.

'You escaped then?' he asked.

'I'm sorry?'

'You escaped from Hinge and Bracket?

'Oh, I see … yes. Is this common?'

'Once they had a milkman in there for two days. The police had to go in in the end. They 're weirdos, you know.'

'Who – the police?'

'No, next door. You never see 'em.'

'And what's it to you?'

'What did you say?'

'You heard me. Why don't you just leave them alone.'

'I've a good mind to ring your supervisor.'

'You don't have a good mind, mate. Minds like yours are too busy thinking the worst of everyone. So why don't you do us all a favour and go in?'

'I've never been so insulted in my life.'

'You want to get out more then.'

As the man scurried back to his hole I got in the van and started up the engine. Before I set off, I glanced back at the house. At one of the windows on the ground floor I could see Dorothy looking out. I waved, but I'm not sure if she saw me or not. Her gaze seemed to be fixed somewhere in the distance.

29

Salty Joe

There is a very odd man I see from time to time as I drive around. He's quite tall, in his mid-sixties, and wears the most bizarre assortment of clothes. I have no idea what he does and where he lives – if he indeed has a home. All I do know is that he does not like deliverymen.

Over the past couple of years the only interaction we have had is the raising of his middle finger as I pass by.

I dedicate this to him.

* * * *

I was in Buckingham again this week - the town centre, to be precise. I don't like delivering in town centres. Not many of us drivers do: too much traffic, no parking spaces, too many disapproving glares from the general public for getting in their way. Add all this to the fact that I was delivering to a student BEFORE midday on a Sunday and you may begin to understand my concerns.

Would they be up? Would they still be drunk from the night before?

I tried not to think about it too much as I parked up and jumped out. As I did so, I became aware of music – well, of a sort. A matter of feet away from the address in question was a busker sitting on a small beer crate.

'Salty Joe' is a bit of a local character, to say the least. No doubt, to the rest of the public he seems like a happy-go-lucky-type, an integral part of the social fabric. I beg to differ.

Salty has an accordion. A very loud accordion. I suppose this was how the trouble all started. You see,

as I attempted to rouse the student in question on the intercom, I couldn't hear a thing. Salty was just so loud.

'OH THE FISHERMAN FISHES THE OCEAN WIDE! HE GETS QUITE CHILLY ON A WINTER MORN'!'

'Excuse me, mate?'

Due to years of accordion abuse, not to mention loud, dreadful singing, Salty has become quite deaf. I tried again.

'EXCUSE ME!'

The accordion slurred to a stop.

'You talkin' to me?' he muttered in a strong Cornish accent.

'Yes. Sorry. I'm just trying to speak to someone. Could you just stop for a few seconds?'

Fixing me with an evil glare, Salty put down his accordion and began to roll a cigarette. As he did so, I took in his strange attire for the first time – a purple three-piece suit covered in so many metal badges the weight was affecting his posture; an orange beret, again covered in badges; and, to finish off, very long cowboy boots. It was a strange combination.

Thanking him, I returned my focus to the intercom. Buzz. Buzz. Buzz. I must have been buzzing for five minutes. But just as I was about to give up I heard a click.

'Hello?' I said, excited by the prospect of moving on.

'Yes?' said a bleary voice. 'What do ya want?'

'Oh, you're in ... great. I've got ...'

'OH THE DOG DOES BARK ON A WINTER'S NIGHT! HIS TAIL IS COLD JUST LIKE HIS AR -'

'EXCUSE ME!'

Once again, the accordion died in Salty's hands. And once again he was fixing me with a glare.

'Sorry. I'm just talking to someone. Could you just stop again for a few seconds?'

'I gave you five minutes.'

'Yes, but it's a student. You know what they're like,' I said, in a hushed tone. 'Hello?' I repeated, returning my focus to the intercom. Nothing. 'Hello – are you there?' Nothing again. 'Oh, bugger. He's gone now!'

'I see,' muttered Salty, glaring at me even more intently. 'Are you a Manchurian?'

'What? Do you mean a Mancunian?'

'I know what I mean. I was mugged in Manchester a few years ago. The accent still haunts me.'

Unless he was mugged by a scrap metal collector, I found his story hard to believe.

'Wasn't me, mate. I haven't mugged anyone for years,' I said, with a feeble laugh. Salty, clearly not impressed by my attempt at humour, continued to glare, forcing me back to my buzzing.

'Hello?' said the voice on the intercom again.

'Oh, hello. Mr Taylor? Sorry about that. I've got a delivery …'

'OH, THE MILK DOES CURDLE, LIKE MY SWEET, SWEET LOVE!'

'COULD YOU PLEASE SHUT UP!'

As Salty stopped once more and everything became silent, I became aware of people staring at me all along the High Street.

'What did you say?' said the voice on the intercom.

'Oh – no, I didn't mean you! I was talking to someone else.'

'Oh,' the voice mumbled, clearly not impressed. 'Did you say you wanted Mr Taylor?'

'Yes, please.'

'You're too late, mate. He moved out a week ago.'

'But I've got a delivery for him.'

'Nothing to do with me.'

Suddenly there was a click ... and then silence.

Frustrated anger bubbling inside, I turned to see a very broad smile on Salty's face. Vainly attempting to hide my embarrassment, I walked back to the van. But as I did the music struck up once more.

'OH, THE MANCHURIAN HAS WASTED HIS TIME ON A SUNDAY MORN'! SERVES HIM RIGHT SHOULD HAVE STAYED UP NORTH IN THE LAND OF THE MUGGERS!'

Just as Salty has a dislike for 'Manchurians', I now have one for accordions.

30

Swing Low, Sweet ... Charlton?

One night a few months ago I nearly delivered to the wrong house. For obvious reasons the lady who opened the door was surprised to see me. But not as surprised as I was. She was wearing a baby doll nightie and high heels.

But that was only part of my surprise. You see, although she didn't recognise me, I most certainly recognised her. I know her name. I know where she lives. And I know her husband.

I just wonder what her husband would have said if I'd told him she was in another man's house in another town while he was away on a stag weekend?

Don't worry though, I don't do blackmail. But I do do funny stories.

* * * *

I had an FTD (First Time Delivery) on Wednesday night. The address in question was Holt Farm, on the outskirts of Charlton, a village in Buckinghamshire. I'd never been there before, and because of this it took me a while to find it. When I finally did, I found the yard packed with cars and music blaring from the large horseshoe-shaped house.

The order was quite large, so I decided to find out exactly where it was to be delivered before I unloaded it. The racket from inside the house was so loud I had literally to bang on the front door with my fist, all to no avail. Deciding I may have a bit more success at another door, I traipsed off into the darkness. Eventually, I found a small doorway at a quieter part of the house. Not wanting to waste any more time, I went on in. There I

found a black priest on a mobile phone, sitting at a kitchen table.

'Things are really hotting up now, Frank, so don't be too long. Oh, and could you bring some spare batteries?'

As he closed the phone, he noticed me.

'Oh, hello. A deliveryman. Now, that *is* original.'

'Sorry?'

'You're a bit late, aren't you?' he said, slurping at a large glass of wine.

'Yes. Sorry. I had a few problems finding you.'

'Oh? This is your first time, is it?'

'Yes, but I'll remember in future.'

'Excellent. Are you on your own?'

'Yes,' I said, slightly bemused.

'Naughty,' he said, with a mock frown. 'That's against the rules. But I suppose it does even things up a little. Between you and me, I think we're a bit female heavy. Fancy a drink?'

'I shouldn't really. But I suppose one little glass won't do any harm.'

'Good man,' he said, standing up and walking around the table. 'Anyway, good to meet you. I'm Peter.'

As I took the glass from him, I stared down at his bottom half in absolute disbelief. It's not every day you see a priest dressed in stockings, suspenders and high heels.

'Come on, then. I'll introduce you …'

'I think you may be getting the wrong end of the -'

'Now, none of that. I know what it's like first time. I was a bag of nerves when I went to my first party.'

'But -'

'But nothing,' he said, grabbing me by the arm and leading me into the house. 'Let you hair down. Live a little.'

As we walked into the hall I was amazed to see a naked elderly white woman run past us, chased by a Roman centurion.

'Hello, darling!' she said.

'Hello, sweetie!' said Peter. 'That's Jennifer. My wife. You see, we do things a little differently here. We like to get into character. It's so much more exciting that way.'

'Look, I think I need to explain something -'

'Portia! William!' Peter shouted, drowning out my voice.

I glanced up to see a naked middle-aged couple descending the stairs. I tried to look away. It wasn't easy. William was a small, well-endowed gentleman in his mid-fifties, whilst Portia was slightly older, with extraordinarily large breasts that swung low across her belly.

I was so shocked I was rooted to the spot.

'Hello, Peter,' said William. 'Is Jennifer with you?'

'You've just missed her. Henry's just chased her towards the living room.'

'Henry from accounts?'

'No. Henry the estate agent from Brackley.'

'Don't think I've had the pleasure.'

'I have,' said Portia, with a smile. 'And who's this?' she added, smiling in my direction.

'Sorry,' said Peter, 'this is...'

'Lee,' I muttered, nervously.

'Would you like to mark my card?' she said.

'What?'

'My card,' she repeated, passing me a piece of paper.

It was warm. God knows where she kept it. I didn't see her carry it down the stairs. When I looked at it, I saw a list of names.

'I've got a little slot around ten.'

If she had a little slot, I was Little Red Riding Hood.

'Do you need a pen?' she asked.

I didn't like to think where she kept that, so I decided it was time to explain my reasons for being there.

'Look, I've got a delivery to make – now, if you'd just tell me where you want me to put it.'

'Oh, bravo!' said Peter, passing the paper back to Portia. 'You two can have him later. He's mine for now,' he added, pulling me down the hall. 'That's the spirit! That was very good. Have you done a lot of role-play? If you can keep that up, you'll be very popular here, I can tell you.'

I was just about to yank my arm from his grasp, when he opened the living room door and pulled me through. There I saw Henry the estate agent (cum centurion) snogging Peter's wife, a partially-dressed cowboy on top of a nun, a policeman straddling a gorilla, and, to my utter astonishment, a topless schoolmistress caning a caveman over on a sofa.

I decided then that enough was enough.

'Right, that's it! How dare you put me in this situation! How could you be so brazen as to organise a delivery when you're having a swingers' night! Look at you all. Swapping your partners willy-nilly. I wouldn't share my lawn mower, let alone my wife! Have you got no shame?'

'Take it easy, old boy,' said Peter. 'I think you're laying it on a bit too thick now.'

'And you can shut up, Desmond Tutu!'

'Who are you?' asked the schoolmistress. Everyone was staring at me now.

'I'm the deliveryman, love! Now, if you can tell me where the owner is and keep your hands off me while I do my job, I just might not report you to my employers.'

'I am the owner,' she said, pointing the cane at me. 'And I don't recall ordering any groceries.'

'Mrs Berry?' All I got was a shake of the head. You could have heard a pin drop. 'Holt Farm?' I gulped.

'Holt House,' she said, advancing on me slowly. 'Holt Farm is a couple of miles down the road.'

'Ah. Right,' I stammered, backing towards the door and glancing at my watch. 'Is that the time? Better be off!'

31

The Confessions of a Deliveryman

So there it is. Take from it what you will. I'm afraid I don't have the answer to the meaning of life, or the key to eternal happiness. All I know is that from my tiny vantage point I have found what is important. That life is what you make it and that the grass is rarely greener over the other side of the fence. I deal with the pressure of life by making up stories. It's a way out. A release when everything gets too much. It works for me. You may find something different. But remember, it's all about scale. Keeping it in perspective.

I only hope from my mid-life experience you may have learnt something. Even if you haven't, I hope it's raised a smile. It has for me. Published or not.

The End

About the Author

Lee Ball grew up in Walkden, Manchester and studied drama at Queen Margaret College in Edinburgh. He now lives in Brackley, Northants with his wife, Sarah and their two children.

If you would like to follow the adventures of the deliveryman and be updated with further publications, please go to:
http://thedeliverymandiaries.blogspot.com/

CPSIA information can be obtained at www.ICGtesting.com
263136BV00001B/18/P